IN THE MIDST OF THE STORM

They Call Me Stormi

A Novel

FELECIA POOLÉ

Published and Distributed By
Stormii Girl Publishing
Compton, California 90221
909-215-4773
Email: theycallmestormi@gmail.com
www.theycallmestormi.com
Cover design: TWA Solutions

Third printing: July 2016
978-0-9978287-0-2
109876543

Library of Congress Control Number: 2014937519

Publisher's note

For inquiries, contact the author at: theycallmestormi@gmail.com

Dedication

This book is dedicated to my children, who I love with all my heart. To my late daughter, Caila. To my oldest son Greggory, and to my youngest son, Khristopher and his wife Mary Jane. To my grandchildren who give me so much joy, Taliyah, Caila, Cali, Trasón, and Trinity and to my two soon-to-be born grandchildren. To Timothy Alonzo Watson (Big Tim) my **soulmate** who provided me with a special place to write.

ACKNOWLEDGEMENTS

The completion of this book has been a long time coming. It could not exist without the many people who encouraged me along the way.

I would like to thank God first and foremost for giving me the strength to push through my first novel. I want to thank my mother, Mrs. Earnestine Poolé-Anderson for always having my back and praying me through to the finish of this novel. My father, Keelo Poolé for his love and support. My siblings Mickoyan, Michael, Anita, Veronica, and Mandrake (Diggie Docc) for always loving and supporting me in all of my adventures, my many nieces and nephews, aunts and uncles, cousins and the remainder of my family and my close friends.

Special thanks, to my "Ride or Die" friends Jewel Puckett, Adrienne Russell, and Tina Johnson Robinson for always being there for me, and my mentor and friend of thirty years Treva Metoyer.

Chapter One

Had I cheated death? Had my survival changed the course of my family's destiny? Had my birth altered the atmosphere? My body was here in the natural, but who was I in the spiritual?

The devil should have drowned me when he had the chance!

At age twelve, you become accountable for your sins. As a young girl, your body begins to change, you become curvier, you gain weight on your hips, and your breasts start to develop. At age thirteen, your menstrual cycle starts, your body is capable of reproducing and you have to decide if you want to wear Kotex or Stayfree Maxi pads.

Instead of being concerned with my changing body, I was lying on a dirty mattress with my legs in the air!

I came into this world fast; I was born at home! My mother delivered me on the toilet. The devil led her to believe I was some shit! The Holy Spirit unction my mother to reach down and save me before my newly crowned head hit the water. The devil had put a hit on me! He would have drowned me at birth, but the Lord saw fit to save me! I was born fighting for my life. Little did my mother know there would be a continuous struggle for my sanity. The devil could not drown me, but he would torment me.

There was a storm the day I was born, so my father nicknamed me Stormi. There was no record of my birth. There was no birth certificate. Even though the devil's attempt to drown me was unsuccessful, I still didn't exist. *I was nobody!* How fucked up was this!

How did I move through life without a birth certificate? What was my God-given name? Did my father understand what he was doing when he nicknamed me Stormi? Did he realize that a storm was a disturbance of the atmosphere, a serious disturbance of any element of nature, a disturbed or agitated state, a sudden or violent commotion, a tumultuous outburst?

My declared nickname set the stage for my rollercoaster life. It set the stage for the making of a mad bitch.

They call me Stormi.

Chapter Two

𝔈

*L*ife happened quickly for me. I was born at the speed of a bowel movement, I walked at seven months, and I spoke complete sentences at ten months, so it was inevitable that at age thirteen I would be laying on my back with my panties at my ankles, anticipating getting my cherry popped!

At five-foot-six, one hundred five pounds, I was tall and thin. People would tell me that I had the height and facial features to be a model, but I did not see it that way. What I saw when I looked in the mirror were my flaws — a light skinned, flat-chest chick with pimples, thick eyebrows and a flat ass. There was nothing special about me, so I thought. I suffered from low self-esteem, so I felt the need to do things for acceptance. People mistook me for being older. I learned early to use this to my advantage. In this life, you have givers and you have takers. At age thirteen, I was a giver. I had the need to please, but through hurt and pain, I learned to be a taker. Unbeknownst to me, this would be my introduction to depression and Multiple Personality Disorder, just to name a few.

I came from a large family. Both my parents were entrepreneurs. My father owned and operated a construction company and my mother was a real estate agent. My father built the houses and my mother sold them. My father had other children from other unions. His "Pole of Life" had been around. We all grew up together as one big happy family. My parents were strict. They raised us with good manners. We answered with "yes, ma'am" and "no, ma'am." We were very polite and everyone was impressed with how well behaved we were. Both from the South, my parents were raised in God-fearing homes, so, of course, we went to church.

By the time I was thirteen, my father stopped attending church. My father loved God, but the Holy Ghost hoes loved my father. I witnessed several women in the church approaching my father when my mother was not around. The things they would do to get his attention were just shameful. One woman gave my father her big-ass panties. I wished I could stop going to church, but my mother would have never let that happen. I hated that I had to be polite to those fake-ass church people. I went to school with some of their children and the stories they told about their parents were mind blowing. These so-called Christians smoked weed and had sex with each other.

They jumped and shouted on Sunday and committed sin Monday through Saturday. I guess this was why they were up early Sunday morning seated in the front row. They needed God to forgive them for their sinful nature. They say God is a God of second chances!

Well not all people in the church were full of shit. Take my mother, for instance. She had a direct line to God. My father always said, "If you want a prayer to get through, have your mother pray."

My mother was a saved, Holy Ghost-filled, beautiful, brown-skinned woman, with an infectious smile, a nice shape, big, beautiful legs and a heart of gold. She grew up in church; her faith and trust in God was immeasurable. She was so amazing.

My father was very smart and articulate. He was what Blacks call mixed—German and Black. Growing up, he had a hard time. He wasn't white enough for Whites and he wasn't black enough for Blacks. My father was a large supporter of the Black Panther Party. *Power to the people!*

We moved to Corona, California in 1970. I was eight years old. We had the only custom-built home on the block. My parents did okay to have six children—Matthew was the oldest, Miles was next, and then me, Stormi, Anastasia was the fourth child, Valencia was the fifth, and Derrick was the sixth. They had many mouths to feed, but we never wanted for anything. The neighborhood was comprised of middle class families—mostly young couples raising at least two or more children. Everyone was friendly and watched each other's children. If we got out of hand, they had no problem chastising us.

I had the biggest crush on James who lived around the corner. He lived with his mother and sister; he was the only son. He was four years older than I was, and we had known each other since I was in elementary school. James was of average height, light complexion, a slim brother who knew how to dress and, for some reason, always had money!

When he would drive down my street in his car, he would stop and talk to me. I got goose bumps every time I saw him. One day, I was sitting on my front porch, and he and a couple other boys from the neighborhood were walking down the street. He stopped and asked me how I was doing. I told him I was doing well. He stood at the bottom of the steps. When my father renovated the house, we had to walk up several steps before we made it to the front door. James asked me to come to the bottom of the steps.

When I got up to walk to the end of the steps, James stared at me. The closer I got to him the more my walk changed. My body had a mind of its own. I walked seductively, swaying my hips that were covered with some very short shorts. James was staring me up and down.

"Stormi you're not the same little girl I remember from elementary school. You're all grown up. I love your thick wavy hair, and you have beautiful legs."

I smiled so hard, I was sure he saw all thirty-two of my teeth. I could have listened to him compliment me all day long. It felt good!

When James got ready to leave, he asked, "Can I have your telephone number?"

I didn't know what to say. I wasn't allowed to receive calls from boys.

My father ran his construction business from the house, so my parents had installed two lines: one for business and the other for personal use. My brothers could talk on the phone to girls, but—even though I could not receive calls—I gave him the number anyway. The fact that I was out of school for the summer, and my parents left for work early in the morning allowed me to talk to him while they were gone.

James called me at twelve o'clock noon every day, giving me enough time to get my housework done and to make sure my younger sisters and brother had done their work as well. We would talk for at least an hour. Every time we talked, James would give me a compliment. He made me feel special. He always told me what he liked about me.

I had bad acne, so I never thought I was pretty. I used Noxzema on my face every day. I was built straight up and down; nothing special, but he always found something he liked about me. Especially my legs, very strong shapely legs just like my mothers.

One day while talking on the phone with James, he told me, "You have nice tits, just enough."

Just enough for what?

"Stormi, you have a model's body. You're tall with nice, long legs. You may want to consider modeling for a career. I think you have what it takes to be a model."

"Not with this acne."

"Your face will clear up. You're pretty and mature for your age. You don't look like you're thirteen. You look much older. We have a lot in common; I enjoy talking to you on the phone. Do you think you are ready for a boyfriend?"

"Yes, I am ready, but I don't think my parents are. They have told me no dating until I am fifteen."

"You will be fourteen in a couple of months. I can't wait a year for you to turn fifteen. I want you as my girlfriend now. We can be together without your parents knowing. What do you think?"

"I think if my parents find out, I'm going to be in a lot of trouble, but I'm willing to take the chance. How are we going to make it work?"

"We will find a way to make it work."

"Well, okay, I guess."

"We have to make it official."

"Huh? What are we going to do, have a ceremony?" I laughed. "James, are you going to get me a promise ring?"

There was a long silence on the phone.

"James, are you still there?"

"Yes Stormi, I'm still here. I was just thinking about the ring. I have to save my money. I should be able to purchase it in about two months, but in the meantime, we need to come together as one."

"What are you talking about, James? I was joking about the ring. What do you mean by come together as one?"

Without hesitation, he replied, "We need to get down."

"Do what?"

"Girl, you know what I'm talking about, the nasty! Have you done it before?"

"*No,* I have not."

"That's good, because it should be with someone special. I will make it special for you and we will become **Soulmates.**"

"I'm not sure I'm ready for that. Maybe we should slow down."

"Look, Stormi, trust me. It will be okay. Just relax and let me lead the way. I promise you, you will enjoy the ride. I'm going to teach you all about your body."

"What are you talking about, James? How are you going to teach me about me?

"I'm going to train you to respond to your own touch. Before I can touch you, you have to touch yourself. You need to know how to make your pussy sing."

"I don't know if I'm ready for that. Why would I touch myself down there?"

"Stormi, are you telling me you have never touched your pussy?"

"James, I prefer that you refer to my private part as a jewel box. The word pussy sounds so nasty, and no, I have never played with myself."

"Girl, you can call it what you want, but until you learn self-satisfaction, you will be lost."

"Okay, tell me what I need to do."

"Call me when everyone has gone to sleep and I will tell you what to do."

"Okay."

I called him in the middle of the night, when everyone in the house was asleep. He answered the phone and the first thing that came out his mouth was, "Take yo' panties off."

My heart started to beat so fast; one because I was excited, and two because I shared a room with my two sisters and the fear of them waking up was making me crazy! I followed his instructions.

"Suck on your index finger and get it good and wet, then spread your legs and take your wet finger and stroke the inner part of your jewel box, and take your other hand and rub your nipples."

Well, the first time was just too awkward; it didn't work for me. I could not get the rhythm. James insisted that I call him every night and practice until I got what he called a *nut!* Finally, after two weeks of practice, it happened. There was an explosion in my body. I wanted to scream, but I couldn't for fear of waking my sisters. I felt the wetness between my thighs, my nipples were hard, and my eyes rolled to the back of my head, he heard me panting on the phone. "You finally got it," James shouted.

If I can do this to myself and it feels this good, I can't wait for James to touch my jewel box, I thought.

James called me the next day with so much excitement in his voice.

"Stormi, I felt like a proud teacher. I know you enjoyed that mind-blowing experience. It's time for the real pipe. I'm going to make you a woman... Let's meet at Lisa's house in an hour."

"Why are we meeting there?"

"We can't meet at your house, and we can't meet at mine. We need to spend some time together. It's time for me to have some fun with your jewel box; you can't have all the fun." He chuckled. I have always considered myself grown. I cooked, cleaned, and took care of my brothers and sisters. At an early age, my father taught me how to drive a car; I ran small errands for my mother. I had done everything adults had done. So naturally, making love or doing "the nasty", as James called it, was just another part of playing grown up.

Lisa and her family lived in the neighborhood for years until her father got a promotion on his job and he moved the family to another state. The house was catty-cornered across from mine. Since Lisa's family had moved, the house was empty. I never imagined my first time would be in a vacant house.

Timing was perfect; my parents were gone. I was the only one at home. *I can't believe I'm getting ready to do this.* James was going to make me a woman! I got very nervous and my heart started beating fast, so I got on my knees to pray. I asked the Lord to take away my fear.

I wanted everything to be just right, so I took a bath. I wanted my jewel box to be zestfully clean! James loved my legs, so I made sure I wore the shortest shorts I had, matching them up with a white back-out blouse. I didn't wear a bra. I wanted him to see my nipples.

We met at the vacant house. It was locked up tight, every door and window locked. We could not get in. I saw the frustration on James' face. He got a rock and broke the windowpane on the kitchen door, reached in and unlocked the door. I was sure this was breaking and entering. *My parents will kill me if they find out about this.* I wanted to go back home and forget this even happened. It was too late; James had opened the door.

"Ladies first" He said.

We entered the house and I looked around. It was dusty and dirty, nothing left but an old, dirty mattress on the living room floor.

I asked James, "Where should I sit?"

"Sit on the mattress."

I yelled, "It's dirty!"

"A little dirt won't hurt."

I was disgusted with the thought of making love on that mattress. That was not how I envisioned my first time. My surroundings were horrible.

"Stormi, what's wrong?"

"I just thought my first time would be different, this place is dusty and dirty, and we have no running water."

"Okay Stormi, you don't have to do this. I thought you were mature enough to handle this, but I guess you're not. We discussed this in the beginning and you said you were ready for a boyfriend. Well this is what comes with it."

Disappointment was all over his face.

"Okay, I am ready. I just wanted my first time to be in a much nicer place."

James assured me that the next time would be much nicer. He told me to pull down my panties. I stood up and removed my shorts, and placed them on the mattress so that I had something shielding my butt from the dirt. I sat down and pulled my panties down to my ankles. Then, the strangest thing happened. I felt a cold wind blow across my naked bottom and my body started to shake.

"Did you feel that?"

"What are you talking about?"

"Did you feel the cold wind blow?"

James got a little irritated. "What wind? We are inside the house and it's the middle of summer. I didn't feel anything. We don't have all day, stop acting silly."

As I sat half-naked on that dirty mattress, I watched him pull his pants down to his knees and hold his erect pole of life in his hand. He wrapped his hand around it and stroked it as if he was shooting dice, and it got bigger and bigger. It looked like a big long one-eyed snake. Something deep down inside me made me feel like I should wait. He got on top of me and forced me to lie down.

"Wait," I said, but he was all over me.

There was no caressing or any kissing just his pole of life poking me in the thigh. He moaned and groaned as he moved his butt up and down. *Wow, is this it? I'm not sure, but I don't think he's in the right spot.*

"This doesn't feel right; I don't think you're in the right spot."

"I know what I'm doing"

He sucked on his index finger, stuck it inside my jewel box, and finger banged me until I was wet.

"You're ready! Now spread your legs wide." He instructed.

As I lay on my back, with my legs in the air, I took a good look at my legs…very statuesque.

I started to see my beauty, and I thought to myself, *you deserve better than this.* There was no way I should have been laying on that dirty mattress. I tried pushing him off me, but he continued to thrust and thrust until his body felt like it weighed a ton. His pole of life was at the entrance of my jewel box, getting harder and harder. He moved faster and faster until he made his entrance.

The shock to my young body was unimaginable. I screamed, but sound did not escape me. It was a silent scream! I felt the cold wind blow again. *God is that you? Did you come to rescue me?* I was in shock; the pain was unbearable. His face appeared distorted; he looked like he had just had a stroke. I felt nothing but pain! My eyes filled with tears. I wanted to cry out to God for help, but the pain silenced me.

My jewel box felt like it was on fire. He was in and out of me in all of five minutes, but it felt like a lifetime. He rolled off me, and onto the dirty mattress, panting like a dog. I sat up, holding my legs together, trying to ease the pain. He wore a smirk on his face. As I stood up blood ran down my legs. I was horrified from the sight of blood. I thought my period had started.

"Look, I'm bleeding!"

"Girl, calm down. You're okay. You just got your cherry popped! Put your shorts on so we can go."

There was no running water, no towels. I couldn't clean myself up. I felt like he had just spit inside me. I used my panties to stop the blood from running down my legs. What just happened? He broke me in as a skilled equestrian breaks in a wild horse.

James pulled up his pants. He slapped me on the butt and smiled at me with a sense of accomplishment.

I, on the other hand, felt like I was in the *Twilight Zone*.

"It's time to go. Stormi, you go first and I will leave a little later. We don't want anyone to see us leaving together."

He walked me to the door and told me to give him a call later.

Very slowly, I walked across the street to my house; feeling like the life had been zapped out of me.

Faced with the reality of what just happened—fucked in an abandoned house—I ran some warm water in the tub. As I sat in the tub soaking my swollen jewel box, I could not stop the tears from streaming down my face. I repeatedly envisioned James and his one-eyed snake thrusting in and out of me, beating up the walls of my virgin womb!

They call me Stormi.

Chapter Three

It was early Sunday morning; I had to get ready for Sunday school. I didn't feel like myself. I didn't get enough sleep. I tossed and turned all night. I called James at our set time, but he did not answer the phone. I dozed off and woke up, and called him again, and still no answer. That was strange. I had spoken with James every night for the past two weeks and now he was not answering the phone.

My sister, Anastasia, pulled the covers off me. "Mom said, 'get up.' You are always the last one to get ready."

"Get the hell away from me," I yelled. "You get on my nerves."

"Ooh, you just said a curse word. I'm going to tell Mommy on you."

She headed straight to the door. I jumped up to stop her.

"Okay Asia, I'm sorry, but you need to stop playing."

My father nicknamed her Asia when she was born, because she looked like an Asian baby. She had tight eyes and light skin with her see-thru look-in ass.

"You cursed at me and I'm going to tell Mommy on you."

I had to plead with that girl for five minutes not to tell. Finally, when I promised to take her to hang out with me, she stopped. I didn't have time for her; she was always getting on my nerve!

I dreaded going to church. It was an all-day affair. I was not up to going, but there was no way my mom was going to let me stay home. It was first Sunday and we had to take communion. My mother was one of the Sunday school teachers, so we had to get there early. Thank God, I was not in her class.

My mom came in the room and told me I needed to wear white, letting me know that I would be attending a special Sunday school class for the youth girls ages thirteen to eighteen. My focus was not on going to church. I was concerned that I had not spoken to James. He should have called by now. I pulled myself together and got dressed. I hoped to see James at church, his mother and his sister where members and he attended on occasion.

When I arrived at Sunday school, I saw my friends, Brandy and Chloe. We have been friends since elementary school. Our parents hung out together. Brandy was a very pretty girl with a style all her own; she loved fashion. Chloe was a lot of fun; she kept everyone laughing.

Of course, we sat in the back of the class. Chloe started making jokes about everyone being dressed in white as soon as we sat down. She told one girl she looked like a big cloud and everyone started to laugh.

Brandy didn't think the joke was funny. She told Chloe that she was being immature. Brandy tried to act as if she was older than everyone else. She had this odd relationship with her parents. They allowed her to do things according to her maturity level. She was fourteen and she dated a nineteen year old... She was the only child and she ran over her parents.

I wished I had that same relationship with my parents. It would have made my life much easier; sneaking around with James was stressful. I definitely had the maturity level to date, but my parents never saw it that way.

Chloe asked me if I knew what the class was about, and I told her I had no idea.

Brandy says, "It's a purity class; we will learn what it takes to stay pure, after which we will make a commitment to the Lord and receive gold rings to wear."

I was trying to comprehend what Brandy just said. My mother didn't mention anything to me about this. We sat in the back listening to Brandy explain what was about to take place.

"What happens if you don't want to make the commitment?" Chloe asked.

"What do you mean, why wouldn't you?" Brandy replied.

"Is there something you need to tell us Chloe?"

"No," Chloe replied. "I'm fourteen years old. I'm not going to commit to something I'm not sure I can do. That's it. I do not intend on playing with God! My cousin told me if you make a promise to God and you renege on it you will burn in hell! I'm not going to hell for a promise I made at fourteen that I may not be able to keep."

Chloe had my full attention. What she said made a lot of sense. I was on Chloe's team and I would side with her when the time came.

"Whatever Chloe, your cousin sounds stupid!" Brandy looked at Chloe with such distain.

"Do you have a problem with my decision, Brandy?"

"Yes, I do, I think you are doing this for attention, you are so immature."

"Oh yeah, I forgot you're the mature one Brandy, that's right you get to do things according to your maturity level. Your parents think you are so mature, that is why they let you date. You have everyone fooled, but I know you, there is no way a nineteen-year-old would be dating you if he were not getting the jewel box. Unlike you, I'm still a virgin!"

Brandy was very upset. "You know nothing about me," Brandy replied. "You assume I have to give up the jewel box. That's the difference between you and me. I'm a lady at all times. My boyfriend is with me because he likes me and that's all. I don't have to lie on my back."

I think they forgot we were at church, as the conversation had gotten heated. I was trying to listen to what Sister Williams was saying and trying to hear what my two friends were saying to each other. I heard a small portion of what Sister Williams said. She spoke about a hymen, and it being the covering the Lord gave a woman. She said something about it staying intact made you a virgin. Sister Williams explained, "It's natural to want to express your love for the opposite sex in a physical way, but you also know God wants you to remain sexually pure in both actions and your thoughts. It's important to save yourselves for marriage. Your husband is the only person you should sleep with, and the first time with your husband will establish your blood covenant."

I wanted to ask questions, but I didn't want anyone assuming anything about me. I just kept quiet and tried to focus on what Sister Williams was teaching.

My heart was beating so fast. I didn't know what to think. I didn't know that my jewel box was a big deal. I didn't know that I was supposed to wait and give it to my husband. No one explained the significance of my hymen. I didn't even know what a hymen was. I didn't know it was a thin membrane, that covered my external vaginal opening and that this thin layer of skin made me a virgin. Had I kept my jewel box closed, when I got married, I would have a blood covenant with my husband. This information was too late for me. I could not turn back the hands of time. I was no longer a virgin. God have mercy on me!

The class was over and it was time to stand and make our commitment. Sister Williams said, "As I call your name, please come to the front."

Chloe and Brandy were still going at it. Sister Williams gave them the eye and they finally quieted down.

Chloe's name was called first. She got up to walk to the platform. As she moved out of her chair, Brandy said, "I guess you changed your mind, you decided to participate." Chloe walked up to the platform and Sister Williams told Chloe to repeat after her, "I wear this purity ring as a good faith commitment to the Lord to keep my virginity until marriage."

Chloe stood there and nothing came out her mouth. I was sitting on the edge of my seat because if she didn't accept the ring, it would set the stage for me not to accept mine.

Sister Williams repeated herself. Sweat beaded on Chloe's forehead. Finally, after two minutes of silence, Chloe replied, "I believe in God and I have a personal relationship with him, but I'm not ready to make a commitment that I don't know if I can keep. I'm only fourteen and I have no idea what I want to do, but I do know I don't want to lie to God. I'm not going to hell for a commitment I may not be able to keep. This was only a two-hour class. I feel I need more time to think this through."

Sister Williams didn't know what to say, as surely, this was the first time someone had been so vocal. She stood with her mouth opened in total shock. I knew she was looking for the right words. The class was in an uproar. I was so glad Chloe stood up for what she believed. It was sure going to come in handy when she called my name.

Everyone was going crazy, as if Chloe started a revolution against the purity ring. The other girls began to talk to one another and they could see her point, so they were second-guessing themselves. Sister Williams was livid; the class was out of control. Sister Williams was not ready for this, she tried to regain control of the class, but no one was listening to what she had to say. As Chloe proceeded to walk back to her seat, some of the girls gave her five. I believed they didn't want to take the ring either for reasons we will never know, but Chloe gave everyone an excuse not to do it. I was sure she didn't mean for that to happen, but it did, and I was glad about it.

Chloe sat down and the first thing that came out of Brandy's mouth was, "You're a stupid bitch! I can't believe you walked away from committing to God and all these other crazy hoes are going to follow behind you."

"Who are you calling stupid? Stupid is thinking I didn't know about the abortion you had six months ago. Stupid is you making a commitment to God, and you're not a virgin. Stupid is on your face right now." Chloe replied.

The next thing I knew they were throwing blows. They were fighting in Sunday school. This was unbelievable. Chairs were flying in the air, I was trying to break them up, but I couldn't. Sister Williams was screaming for help, but all her little angels were actually instigating the fight. It was crazy; others started to fight—those against what Chloe said versus those believing in what she said. Sister Williams ran out the room to get help.

Brandy and Chloe were on the floor, tearing each other's clothes off. I tried to pull them apart, but every time I tried, I was hit. Sister Williams went to the sanctuary to inform the parents of what was going on. The parents ran into the room and the room filled quickly.

Brandy's mom ran towards her, screaming at Chloe to let her daughter go. Chloe was kicking Brandy's ass. She was sitting on top of Brandy, beating her in the face. Brandy was trying to fight her back.

Brandy's mom punched Chloe in the face with so much force it knocked Chloe off Brandy. Chloe tried to stand up, but Brandy's mom ran over to Chloe and continued punching her in the face. Brandy ran to help her mother... They were beating the shit out of Chloe. They had her on the floor. Brandy lifted her foot to stomp Chloe. I kicked her in her back as hard as I could to prevent her from stomping her.

"Stop hitting her, you're going to kill her." I said.

Brandy's mom continued to hit Chloe. I didn't know what to do. Should I hit an adult, but before I could figure it out, Chloe's mom came into the room like a tornado and knocked the shit out of Brandy's mom. She fell over with blood oozing from her nose. Brandy tried to help her mom, but Chloe's mom grabbed Brandy and threw her into the wall. Oh my God, it was going down at the church. It was pure pandemonium!

As Chloe's mother kneels down to help her get up, she keeps her eyes on Brandy's mother. Brandy's mom gets up, and wipes the blood off her face using the sleeve of her dress. She then walks over and picks a chair up off the floor and propels it at Chloe's mom. The chair barely missed hitting her in the head. She was acting like a mad woman. Chloe's mom stood up and turned towards Brandy's mom, and they both started swinging on each other. Chloe's mom's dress was ripped and her hair was all over her head. She had scratches on her face and hands. I had never seen two adults fight, but I had to give it to Chloe's mom, she was a beast!

Some members from the church ran over and pulled them apart. They were screaming, kicking, and cussing in the church. It was obvious they forgot where they were. Chloe's mom pulled away and ran over to see about Chloe. She tried to help Chloe to her feet, but Chloe could barely stand. She sat down on the floor with her, putting Chloe's head in her lap. Brandy's mom made her way over to Brandy. It was very chaotic. People were everywhere trying to figure out who needed medical attention.

I heard Pastor Lewis over the loudspeaker say: "IN THE NAME OF JESUS." The room instantly silenced. It was as if Jesus himself spoke. Pastor Lewis was appalled at what he had witnessed. He told everyone to move out of the room and make their way to the parking lot.

The police entered with the paramedics. They treated Chloe first; she was badly beaten. The paramedics put her on a gurney to transport her to the hospital. Her mother was walking along side of her as they put Chloe in the ambulance. Chloe's mother got in with her and they left for the hospital.

Brandy and her mother had minor bruises. They were treated at the church. The police questioned everyone about how the fight got started. The next thing I knew, they were arresting Brandy's mother.

I had never experienced anything like that in my life. I couldn't believe what happened. My mother entered the room and pulled me to the side to ask me what happened. I told my mother the story and she couldn't believe that Brandy's mother would jump on Chloe.

Pastor Lewis asked the congregation to meet in the main sanctuary. The commotion didn't stop the service; it just gave the pastor something to preach about.

The call me Stormi.

Chapter Four

✻

*I*t was Sunday evening. As I sat home watching TV, the phone rang. I was hoping it was James. I picked up the phone on the first ring and said excitedly, "Hey, James."

"Girl, it's Shannon. What are you up to?"

"Girl, I thought you were James."

"I see, but no it's just little old me, Shannon. I'm calling to see if you want to come over and listen to music?"

"I have to ask my mother if it's okay."

"Call me back and let me know."

I really didn't feel like listening to music, but I didn't have anything else to do. Waiting for James to call was frustrating. *I might as well go over to Shannon's; listening to music will keep my mind occupied.* I asked my mother if it was okay to go over to Shannon's and she said yes.

Shannon was my best friend. She was very thin, with coco brown skin and long, beautiful hair. She was very easy to get along with, and she had a very bubbly personality. She lived directly across the street from me. We had been friends since elementary school.

My mother gave me permission to go to Shannon's house for an hour.

I knocked on the door, and Shannon's mother let me in.

"Well, hello Stormi, how are you?"

"I'm good, Mrs. Roberts."

"You know where Shannon's room is."

"Thank you, Mrs. Roberts."

I entered Shannon's room and she was dancing around, listening to the Jackson 5. She loved their music.

"Hey Shannon."

"Hey Stormi."

I sat on Shannon's bed, looking at the Jackson 5's album cover; she had a very big music collection. I didn't say much. Shannon could sense something was wrong. I wasn't my usual self.

"What's going on, Stormi? You're not saying much and you're acting weird. This wouldn't have anything to do with what happen at your church today, would it?" Shannon chuckled.

"Yes, it would. Today was a crazy day. I'm actually stressed out."

"What are you stressed about?"

"About our Sunday school class we had to attend today."

"What was the class about?"

"It was about remaining pure until you get married."

"Why would that stress you out?"

"Well, I have something to tell you, but I don't want you to judge me."

"I have been your best friend since elementary school; I love you, I would never judge you."

I wanted to tell Shannon what happened so badly, but I couldn't bring myself to tell her. I couldn't risk taking the chance of being judged, so I changed the conversation.

Two hours had passed and Mrs. Roberts entered Shannon's room to let me know my mother had called, I was supposed to be home an hour ago. Shannon hugged me, as I got ready to leave.

"Everything will be okay Stormi. We will talk later."

I headed home. I wasn't feeling like myself. I should have confided in Shannon. For some reason I felt like I walked differently. I was so paranoid, I just knew my mother could tell by the way I walked that I had sex.

It was time for me to go to sleep; I had a very busy day. I was sure I would feel better in the morning.

I woke up at 2:00 a.m. I was lying in bed wide-awake. I looked at the phone, hoping and praying it would ring. I waited and waited, but no phone call.

Days go by and still no call. I waited by the phone every day. I would sit outside waiting for him to drive down my street, but still no James. I called him for a week straight. I left messages with his sister. He never returned my call. I started to feel depressed, alone, and inadequate. That was when my multiple personalities started to emerge.

Stormi 1 was my softer side. She always wanted to do the right thing. She thought she could pray her way through anything. She was easy going, soft spoken and always talked about the Lord. She had a passion for people.

Stormi 2 would tell it like it is. Her vocabulary was filthy; she would curse you out and feel nothing; she liked to fight and was always looking for revenge. She never slept. She was always on guard. She would cut your throat if she had to.

I didn't know what to do. I hadn't heard from James, so I decided to try to call him one more time. I picked up the phone and dialed James' number. He answered on the first ring.

"Hello"

"Hey James, it's Stormi. How are you?"

"I'm cool. What's up?"

"Nothing's up, I just thought it was strange that I haven't seen or heard from you in a week."

"I've been busy. Let me get back with you a little later, you caught me in the middle of doing something for my mother."

Before I could respond, he hung up the phone. *I didn't understand what was going on with him. Why did he rush me off the phone?*

I instantly felt overwhelmed; my hands started to sweat and my stomach felt queasy. I felt like I wanted to throw up.

Stormi 2: You're not sick. Pull your shit together. You gave up the pussy now he's not trying to be bothered with you. Fuck him. Don't start tripping; this is the game boys play once they get what they want. They move on to the next one. That motherfucka couldn't even find your pussy. Deal with the facts; he got the pussy so he doesn't have to chase you. Trust me, he will call, because he will always want to fuck. That will be your opportunity to pay his ass back.

Stormi 1: Maybe this is for the best. It's okay, you made a mistake, but God loves you. Talk to your mother, she will understand what you are going through. With repentance and prayer, you will make it through this. Don't be afraid to talk it over with your mother, she will understand.

I tried to make sense of what was going on with James. I repeatedly went over in my head what took place from the time he asked me to be his girlfriend. I had a very good memory and I was sure I understood that we were a couple. Maybe it was just as he said, he has been busy, but why did I feel as if he was lying to me.

Stormi 2: Why are you acting so confused? He fucked you and didn't call you for days, and when you decided to call him, he's unavailable. This dude is using you and you can't see it Don't start letting people walk all over you. Care about those who care about you. You need to be more selective on who you fuck.

Another week passed. Finally, he called. Instead of being pissed off, I swallowed my pride, and responded as if nothing was wrong. I was so excited to hear from him. I didn't think he would ever call.

When I answered the phone, he asked, "What are you doing on Saturday?"

"Nothing" I replied.

"Do you think you can get out the house?"

"Yes, I'm sure I can."

"Well, I'm going to a party and I want you to meet me there. Reese and your other friends are going too, so hook up with them so you will have a ride."

"Okay!" I said, excitedly.

I knew my parents would not allow me to go to the party, so I had to start planning how I would get out of the house. My good friends, Joyce and Reese lived on the same block. Joyce was only a year older than I was, but Reese was four years older. Reese was tall and thin with big titties and a small waist with a nice butt. She was what they would call a "Brick House." She was cool! I liked having her as a friend, she was like a big sister.

Joyce was average size — not too thin and not too thick. She liked to hang out and have fun. She lived a few houses down.

We were all at Shannon's house listening to music. Reese was up dancing around, acting crazy.

"Look at my new moves... I will be the life of the party on Saturday. Stormi, are you going to be able to attend the party?"

"I really want to go; I just have to devise a plan to get me out the house."

"Well, I guess we should put our heads together to help you get out," says Reese.

As we sat there, trying to come up with a plan, I felt compelled to let my girls know that I had sex with James.

I said very softly, "I had sex." It got so quiet you could hear crickets chirping.

I had everyone's attention. Reese's eyes got so big they looked like they were going to pop out of her head, but she never said one word. I could see the shock on her face.

Joyce asked, "Well, did it hurt?"

Shannon chimed in, "Wow, Stormi, I would have never guessed, are you okay?"

"No, I'm not okay. Making love for the first time was an indescribable pain. After I gave myself to James, I didn't hear from him for almost two weeks. I felt like he had just fucked me and moved on and to make matters worse, I had to attend a purity class at church where I almost had to make a commitment to God to remain a virgin."

Reese yelled, "Are you serious? Are you talking about James that lives around the corner?"

I yelled back, "Of course! You know I have always liked him. What other James do you know?"

Joyce got up, moved beside me, and started joking around. "Stormi did the nasty! So are you going to do it again?"

"Yes, I'm going to do it again. It wasn't what I expected, but I'm sure it will be better the next time."

Reese yelled, "What! You really plan to do it again. You are just a kid. You should slow down. Girl, James is much older; you can't really believe he's serious about you. I'm not trying to hurt your feelings, but James is not someone you want to give your heart to."

"You were my age when you first did it Reese! So what is your problem? James cares about me. We have already discussed the age difference and we plan on making it work."

"Well, I just think maybe you should take your time," Reese said.

I took a deep breath and blew it out. "Well, it's done, and I'm going to do it again, so can we please work on the plan to get me out of the house?"

Shannon suggested that I stay the night at her house. Her parents played Bid Whist every Saturday night so they would not be home when we got ready to leave. Joyce did not have any suggestions; she kept giggling and asking me a bunch of stupid questions, and Reese didn't say another word. It appeared the only one that was trying to help me was Shannon.

I couldn't wait for Saturday to get here. I made sure I did everything my mother asked of me. Saturday morning I got up the nerve to ask my mother about spending the night at Shannon's house. My mother gave me permission and I was so happy! Later that evening, I was in my room packing my overnight bag in a hurry. I didn't want my mother to see what I was putting in the bag. I had some nice hip huggers and a Cleopatra Jones jacket. It was going to look great together. As soon as I pulled the jacket off the hanger, in walks Asia.

"Why are you putting your jacket in your bag?"

"I'm spending the night at Shannon's and we are going to play dress up."

"Stop lying, Stormi, I already know you're going to a party. Reese's little sister, Tracy, told me. She said Reese asked her mother to use the car and she told her mother who was riding with her and your name was mentioned. Does Mommy know you're going to a party?"

"No, she doesn't and you're not going to tell her."

"Yes, I am."

"Asia, if you tell on me I'm going to tell your friends about those accidents you have in the middle of the night. Now you be a good little sister and go play with Valencia."

Asia stormed out of the room. I had been saving that for Asia for a long time. I knew that information would come in handy. Asia was such a brat. She didn't know it, but I would never tell her secret. Even though she got on my nerve, she was still my little sister.

I finished packing my bag, kissed my mother good-bye, and ran across the street to Shannon's house. I knocked on the door and Shannon's mother opened the door. As I was coming in, Shannon's mother and father were leaving out. I greeted them both with a hello and ran passed them to Shannon's room.

"Hey, girl."

"Hey, Stormi, are you ready for tonight?"

"Yes, I am. I have all my goodies in my bag. Do you have some eyeliner I can use?"

"Yeah, my mother has all types of makeup in her bathroom. Look at my new jeans, what do you think?"

"Girl, those are hot!"

"Thank you! I can't wait for Tony to see me in these. I think they make my butt look big."

"Girl, you're crazy! Who's Tony?"

"I met him at the Corona swap meet. He lives on the eastside of Corona. We have been talking for about a month, I like him a lot, but he hasn't said anything about me being his girlfriend."

"Girl, well take your time. You know what happens when they make you their girlfriend."

"I know, Stormi, but I'm not ready for that. I may play around, but nothing more than that."

"I hear you, Shannon. Sometimes things don't go as you expect and you end up in a situation that you have no control over."

"I understand Stormi. I'm not judging you. I'm just speaking about me."

We lay everything out on the bed so that we could get dressed. I put on my hip huggers; they looked great with my white tied-up blouse. I went to the bathroom to use Mrs. Robert's makeup. She had so much I didn't know where to begin. I decided to use the eyeliner and the mascara.

Shannon walked in wearing her new windowpane jean suit. It was fantastic. She put on her makeup and we were ready to go. Shannon phoned Reese, and Reese told her she was on her way. We stood in the doorway waiting for Reese. She pulled up in her mother's car. We jumped in and we were on our way.

We got to the party. I was so excited, and I couldn't wait to see James. I hadn't seen him since the dirty mattress ordeal. The party was extremely crowded. It was the first party I had attended without my mom taking me.

I knew I looked good. I walked into the party with Reese, Shannon, and Joyce. I barely got in the front door before I was asked to dance. I kindly said, "No thank you."

I was searching the room for James. Reese and Joyce were on the dance floor. Shannon and I continued to walk toward the back of the party. Shannon saw her friend Tony. She introduced him to me. He was a nice looking guy. He grabbed Shannon by the hand and guided her to the dance floor. I felt a little out of place; everyone was on the dance floor except me. I decided that I would dance with the next person that asked. I still didn't see James. I went outside in the backyard and I sat down on a patio chair; I watched my friends party and have a good time.

This nice looking guy came and sat next to me. He introduced himself.

"Hello, my name is Trent. What's your name?"

"My name is Stormi."

"That's an interesting name."

"Yes, I know, there was a rainstorm the night I was born so my father nicknamed me Stormi."

"Well, Stormi, would you like to dance?"

"Sure."

I was having a good time. I danced about three records straight and James still hadn't shown up. Trent was nice and so cute, but I was afraid that if I kept dancing with him he was going to get the wrong impression. I had been at the party well over an hour and James still hadn't shown up.

Stormi 2: Trent appears to be a good dude. I think he may have a little change in his pockets. Stop wasting your time on James' dumbass. I told you he ain't shit. Girl, you had better get with someone who is doing some thangs! James is not concerned about you.

Trent and I sat down and got to know each other better. He told me he was twenty-two. I was shocked. I couldn't believe that a twenty-two-year-old would be interested in me.

I asked him, "What type of work do you do?"

"I'm in the retail business."

"Really, what do you sell?"

"Pharmaceuticals, I can get whatever you want from weed to pills."

"I'm not into drugs."

"Good, then you can sell them and make you some money. What college do you attend?"

Does he really think I'm in college? If I tell him, I will be fourteen at the end of the month I'm sure he will walk away.

Before I could answer the question, Joyce walked up.

"Hello, my name is Joyce and yours?"

"My name is Trent. How are you?"

"I'm good. Are you a friend of Stormi's?"

Trent replied, "I'm trying to be."

Joyce walked over to me and whispered, "I saw James pull up, and Reese is outside talking to him."

I turned to Trent and said, "It was nice meeting you, but I have to go."

Trent handed me a card with his number on it and asked me to give him a call.

Joyce and I headed to the front of the house. James walked in the door and walked right past me. I knew he saw me standing there. In walked Reese right behind him. I didn't understand what happened. What kind of game was he playing? I looked at Joyce and she hunched up her shoulders as if she was clueless to what was going on. I walked behind Reese and tapped her on her shoulder. She turned around and looked at me.

"Stormi, I didn't see you standing there."

"Were you outside with James?"

"Girl, yes, we had to take care of some business. You know James handles the little homies."

My heart was pounding. This motherfucka walked right past me, as if I wasn't there. He couldn't be serious; he asked me to come to the party.

He walked over to his friends and started talking. Reese walked toward the back of the house and Joyce was still standing there with me.

"Stormi, did you see Reese's lipstick? It was smeared across her face. You know Reese's known for giving blow-jobs, I wonder who she just blew."

Joyce was laughing her ass off.

My eyes were filling up with tears. I sat down on the couch and tried to catch my breath. I felt like I was going crazy. I wanted to scream, but I couldn't. I wanted to fuck him up.

Joyce sat next to me. "What's wrong with you, Stormi?"

"Did you just insinuate that Reese just gave James a blowjob?"

"Girl, no, but she probably gave it to one of his friends. She does whatever James tells her to do for the hood..."

I couldn't believe what I was hearing.

Shannon walked over to me and asked, "Are you okay"?

"No! I feel like I'm going crazy. I want to slap the shit out of James. He walked past me as if he didn't see me."

Stormi 2: I told your ass he ain't shit. You need another dude. Stop acting stupid. Stop and listen to what's being said. Joyce knows what's up. I'm sure Reese sucked his dick. She actually told you in so many words. I have a feeling I'm going to have to put this motherfucka on the hit list.

Finally, he walked over to me.

"Stormi, baby, I didn't know that was you. You look different. Damn, girl you look good." He pinched my butt. *Really, motherfucka?* Instead of cursing him out, I said hello like a dumb bitch!

James grabbed me by the hand and led me to the dance floor. I started to loosen up. I forgot what I was mad about, but then Reese walked past and I got mad all over again. I told James what Joyce told me about the blowjobs.

"There is no truth to what Joyce said. Reese is an OG home girl from the neighborhood and I have major respect for her."

For some reason I believed James. We laughed and danced all night. Before the party was over, James and I went to his car. We sat and talked for another hour before James suggested that he get a quickie. I got in the backseat so no one could see us, and I let James handle his business. This time it wasn't so bad!

When it was time to go, we piled in the car with Reese. We went to Zorba's hamburger stand and everyone got a special. We had a great time hanging out. Shannon and I made it to her house before her parents got back from playing Bid Whist.

Now I lay me down to sleep I pray the Lord my soul to keep, if I should die before I wake I pray the Lord my soul to take. As I lay in the bed thanking the Lord before I go to sleep, I breathed a sigh of relief. I had a great time at the party. James danced with me all night, and I felt like it was all about me.

They call me Stormi.

Chapter Five

✼

Hot fun in the summertime! One more week and I would be fourteen. Things are getting better at home. My parents are letting me hang out more. I will be glad when I'm no longer the homely chick on the block.

It was a nice day! All the homies were going to Griffith Park to hang out. Shannon called and asked, "Is your mother going to let you go to the park?"

"I'm sure she is. I just have to let her know with whom I'm riding. You know I can't tell her I'm riding with James."

"Well, tell her you're riding with Reese, and see what she says, because I'm not going if you can't'.

I asked my mother if I could go to the park and I gave her all the pertinent information.

Permission granted! One more lie told to get out of the house. Shannon and I walked down the street to Reese's house.

"Hey Reese, what's up?" I asked.

"Girl nothing, I'm getting ready to go to the park. Are y'all going?"

"Yes, we're going. That's why we're here."

"What do you mean?"

"I need you to drop us around the corner at James' house."

"Damn, you always got other people in your bullshit. Don't always assume that I'm going to help yo' ass."

"Reese, are you having a bad day? I don't understand why you feel the need to speak to me this way, and if it's a problem, Shannon and I will walk."

I listened to her ramble on about how I needed to go sit my ass down somewhere.

Stormi 2: Drop that bitch where she stands. What the fuck are you doing? Did you just hear what she said to you? Hell naw! She got you fucked up. Hit that bitch in the face.

Reese finally stopped complaining.

"I'm going to do it this time, but next time y'all better notify me in advance."

Stormi 2: You make sure you keep an eye on this bitch: something is going on. I just haven't put my finger on it. The time is going to come when you're going to have to deal with her. I believe she's up to something. I'm sure; she's going to be on my hit list.

I was excited to be going to the park. Reese dropped Shannon and me off at James' house. James was standing outside with King, one of the homies from the neighborhood, waiting on us. Shannon and King got into the back seat, and I got in the front seat and sat right under James. This was so cool. We were rolling down the freeway with the music bumping, and everybody was moving to the beat. *(Rollercoaster, of love, say what!)*

Something smelled funny. Smoke was coming from the backseat. I turned around and saw Shannon getting high with King. She motioned to me with the joint in her hand and offered me a hit.

"I'm cool," I said. "I don't get high."

James said, "Puff, puff, pass, girl. Hit that joint. If you're rolling with me then you get high."

Stormi 1: Don't do it, don't defile your temple with that stuff.

Stormi 2: Girl, please! Hit that shit; your temple is already defiled. This will help you relax. It's just weed, and you will see things differently. It makes things much clearer.

"James, that's not for me. I don't want to get high. Someone has to stay sober in case you can't drive back."

He paused for a minute and said, "You're right. Good looking out!"

We arrived at the park and Shannon got out of the car, stumbling.

"Are you okay?" I asked.

"I'm cool."

"Stormi, let's hike up this hill and see how high we can go," James said.

"Okay, give me a minute. I have to make sure Shannon is okay."

"Shannon come on, you're going with us. I think you need to walk it off."

"Go ahead Stormi, I'm cool. I'm not trying to hang with you and James."

"Shannon, it's no problem, we are just hiking up the hill."

King got out of the back seat and said, "She can hang out with me. We'll be right here when y'all get back."

I asked Shannon one more time to go with us.

"Stormi, I'll be okay here with King."

We proceeded up the hill and we made it to the top. We sat on a huge rock and just talked. James was a different person when he wasn't around his friends. He was much nicer; I saw a side of him I did not know existed. He was smart and knew what he wanted out of life. He would be going to college in September. We talked about what he wanted to do when he finished school; he wanted to open up his own business.

I could see a future with him, but now he was telling me he thought we should slow down on the sex. I could not believe what I was hearing. Instead of me just saying okay, I started asking questions.

"What do you mean slow down?"

"I had a long talk with my sister and she feels like I should take a step back. I'm four years older than you."

"I don't understand how your sister found out."

"Stormi, you called my house almost every day. You left several messages for me. She asked me and I told her."

"It sounds like you're breaking up with me."

"I'm not breaking up with you; we have to be careful. You're still my girl. If you call me and I don't answer the phone, don't leave a message. You just have to wait for me to get back with you."

"The last time I waited for you to call me back it took about two weeks."

"Stormi, I had a lot on my mind, but I made it up to you at the party."

"Okay James, as long as we are still together that's good enough for me."

Stormi 2: He is full of shit. His sister told him he is too old to be messing around with you. If someone of authority finds out, he will get in trouble that's what his sister told him. He is a user that's why he fucked you in an abandoned house and in the backseat of a car. This motherfucka can go to jail for messing around with you. Don't trust him.

James grabbed and kissed me and then he pulled me into the bushes for a quickie!

After five minutes of stroking, James and I headed down the hill. When we got back to the parking lot, we did not see his car. We walked around in circles looking for the car. I spotted the car parked under a big shade tree. We started walking towards the car. The closer we got to the car it appeared that someone was in the backseat.

As we approached the car with caution, we looked in the window and saw that Shannon was butt-ass naked in the backseat, and King was fucking her like a Mandingo Warrior. I started beating on the window.

"What are you doing? Get your black ass off her!"

Shannon looked at me with a blank stare. She looked like she had totally zoned out. "What the hell did she smoke?" I said.

James opened the car door and told King to get out. He got out of the car and just stood there naked holding his erect pole of life. James told him to put his clothes on. I could see in his eyes that he was high; they must have smoked something stronger than weed. This fool stood outside the car with a dumbass look on his face, putting his clothes on. I couldn't believe what I was seeing.

"King, I know Shannon didn't agree to this. What did you give her?" I asked.

James started yelling at King. "Man, what did you give her?"

"I gave her a wet one."

"Man, you can't be serious."

I got in the backseat and helped Shannon put her clothes on. I had no idea what happened, but I know my friend and there was no way she would have consented to this.

I didn't know what to do. I was so afraid. James was pacing back and forth. King was leaning on the hood of the car.

"King, we are in trouble. They are minors. What were you thinking? Damn!"

Reese walked up with some friends. "What y'all up to?"

James told Reese what happened.

"What! King what were you thinking?" Reese asked.

"She was down to try it," King said.

Reese got in the back seat with us and began talking to Shannon, but she wasn't responding.

"Stormi, help me get her into my car," she yells.

We got Shannon out of the car. She was falling down, she couldn't walk, and she had white foam around her mouth. I was so petrified, I felt like I was going to pee on myself. We put her into the backseat of Reese's car and I got in with her. Reese was standing outside of the car talking to James.

She got in the car and said, "We're going to get a room at a motel and take care of Shannon."

I shouted, "What are you talking about? We need to take her to the hospital. We are not going to a motel. She needs help!"

"We are getting a room and James is going to get some milk to bring her high down. We will feed her and give her a shower. She will be fine."

"No, you're going to take her to the hospital. She might die! We don't know how much she smoked. I'm not going to be a part of this shit."

Reese reached over the seat, grabbed my face, and held it tight. "Listen little girl, if you don't want your fucking boyfriend and King to go to jail you will do what I tell you to do. We don't snitch."

I had to choose between my boyfriend and my best friend. This was too much. I felt overwhelmed. Everything that could go wrong had. Not to mention I had to be home at a certain time.

James walked over to the car and leaned in through the window.

"Stormi, please do this for me. I can't go to jail and we can't snitch on King."

"James, she needs to go to the hospital."

"Stormi, trust me she will be okay. She needs milk; this will bring her high down."

"I'm scared."

"I'm scared too, but I have been in this situation before. She is going to be okay; just let me get her some milk and something to eat. Okay?"

"Okay, hurry up and make her better!"

Reese found a Motel 6 nearby. We helped Shannon into the room. She was not looking too good. We got her to lie down on the bed, and I climbed into bed with her and put my arms around her. I didn't know what to do. *What would my mom do?* My mother was a prayer warrior. People called her all the time for prayer. She always said, "Prayer changes things."

As Shannon laid on the bed, I began to cry out to God for help. All I could think was she might die. I felt responsible. I had never prayed this hard in my life. Every prayer my mom had ever prayed was coming out of me. My mother always talked about the miracles that Jesus had performed. I begged Jesus to save her.

"Are you serious?" Reese asked. "You really think God's going to help her? All she needs is some milk. Y'all fast asses shouldn't have come anyway. You are too young to hang with us. I keep telling James you are going to get his ass into some trouble."

Stormi 1: Continue to pray, God hears your prayers. She doesn't know the God you serve. Step out on faith. Prayer does change things.

There's a knock at the door. It was James with food and milk for Shannon. I gave Shannon the milk and then

I fed her. It took about an hour, but Shannon was beginning to feel better. Shannon got up to go to the bathroom, and I followed her.

"Do you want to take a shower?" I ask.

She nods yes.

After I helped her into the shower, I got on my knees to thank God for the miracle. I walked out of the bathroom to give her some privacy. James and Reese were sitting together on the bed talking; they seemed a little too cozy for me. I walked over and sat on James' lap. I wanted to thank him for helping Shannon.

"How is she doing?" James asked.

"She's much better. She's taking a shower."

"Damn, that was close. Is she still tripping?"

"No, she's not saying anything. I'm not sure if she remembers what happened."

"Yeah, I spoke with King, and he said she was down with it."

"That's a lie. You know Shannon; there is no way she would have smoked PCP. Your friend is full of shit."

"Whatever, it's over and done."

"It's not over. She has a boyfriend, and I know that she cares for him; it's no way she would have fucked King if she was in her right mind."

I looked over at Reese, and she had this evil smirk on her face.

Stormi 2: You put yourself in a bad position. What would have happened if Shannon died? You have to learn self-preservation. You always come first. Do what works for you and not for everyone else. If people see your weakness, they will use it against you. Remember you owe Reese for grabbing your face. When the time comes, I want you to show her what you're working with.

They call me Stormi.

Chapter Six

Several weeks passed and everything appeared to be back to normal. The incident with Shannon was never mentioned. There was a code in the streets that they lived by—no snitching. It makes me wonder what else this neighborhood had covered up.

It was finally here; the Fourth of July block party. A neighborhood tradition for many years, it was huge. I loved it. All my aunts, uncles, and cousins came over and we had the biggest block party in history! It took a year to plan—good music, food, and fireworks. It was funny to watch all the neighborhood adult men compete. No one wanted to admit it, but it was an unspoken competition. Who would put on the best fireworks show?

Every year, my older cousins would show up with illegal fireworks. The shit they bring would blow up a block. They were real OGs — the ones that roll up in low riders with rags tied around their heads, with their shirts buttoned up as if they were damn near going to choke.

The neighbors got nervous when they saw them and the ones that hadn't spoken to us all year long were now in my parents' face. The shit was funny. I hated fake-ass, scary people.

I called Shannon to see what she was going to wear. We usually dress alike every year, but since the park incident, she had been a little distant. I tried to give her space, but I couldn't help it, I called and checked on her every day, she acted as if everything was ok, but I knew deep down she was suffering.

Shannon didn't answer the phone. I looked out our front window to see if I saw her helping her family set up their tables. I didn't see her, but I did see her parents getting everything set up. She was most likely getting dressed. The streets were packed with people; the entrances had been blocked off. The DJ started playing music, people were dancing in the streets; it was amazing to see everyone having so much fun. I was hanging out with my cousins, laughing and eating.

Joyce and Reese walked down to my house. Everyone knew my parents threw a helluva party. We laughed and played games and ate to our heart's desire. I saw James and some of the other guys from the neighborhood walking towards our house.

My parents thought James and I were just friends, so they thought nothing of it when he and the other guys showed up. It was all about having a good time.

In the crowd, I saw King's ugly ass. *What is he doing at my house? He knows I don't like his ass.* I looked across the street and I still didn't see Shannon. I didn't want her to see him here. I didn't want her to think I invited him to my house.

I walked across the street to Shannon's house and asked her mother where she was. She pointed to the house and said, "Go inside and get her."

I opened the door and called out to her, but she didn't answer, so I proceeded to her bedroom.

"Knock, knock," I called out to Shannon, "I hope you're dressed because I'm coming in." I entered her room and my heart dropped.

Shannon was hanging from the ceiling fan with a rope wrapped around her neck.

"Oh my God!"

I tried to get her down. I got underneath her and tried to take the weight off her neck, but she was too heavy! I was screaming for help, but no one heard me because of the music.

I was scared to leave her, but I had to. I ran out of the house, screaming. "Help me! Help me! Shannon hung herself!"

Shannon's father dropped all the food on the ground and ran inside the house. Her mother was running behind him. My mother saw the panic in my face and ran across the street. We entered the house and Shannon's father had cut her down and had started administering CPR. Shannon's mother was screaming, "My baby! My baby! Lord, save my baby."

My mother was on the floor helping Shannon's dad

with the CPR. As he blew air into her lungs, my mother pushed on her chest. Shannon's face was blue. I didn't see any signs of life.

I got on my knees and began to pray... "Heavenly Father, hear my prayer. Please, Father God, save my best friend's life."

Shannon's father and my mother were still working on Shannon.

My mother kept repeating, "Breathe, Shannon, breathe."

The paramedics entered the house and took over working on Shannon. They got a pulse and started giving her oxygen. The color was coming back into her face. All I could say was, "Thank you Jesus, for saving her."

Shannon was taken away in the ambulance. I was dumbfounded. *My best friend tried to kill herself,* I thought, as I watched the ambulance drive away. I saw King standing in the crowd, and I walked over to him.

"You are a sorry motherfucka! What kind of man has to drug someone to have sex? You ain't shit, and you ain't gon' ever be shit, you had better watch your back, because *you will never know when the Storm is coming your way!*"

"Girl, get away from me with all that bull; I didn't do anything. You need to watch your mouth. You're talking too much. I'm going to let James handle your little ass."

"Fuck you, King."

What a Fourth of July, one I will never forget. Shannon's suicide attempt messed everyone up. Everyone tried to have a good time, but it was hard to do. I needed some space. I got a chair and sat away from the crowd. I couldn't get the picture of Shannon's limp body hanging from the ceiling fan out of my mind.

Reese walked over to where I sat. "How are you doing?"

"I'm not doing well. I can't get Shannon out of my mind. I can't believe she tried to kill herself."

Reese bent down and whispered in my ear. "Don't forget what I told you, we don't snitch! I know it's hard to see your friend on her deathbed, but don't let your feelings make you lose sight of what's important. You are going to have to take one for the hood, because if you don't you just might get fucked up."

"Reese, are you serious? You're still trying to cover this up. What about Shannon, do you even care what's happening with her?"

"Shannon knew what she was getting herself into. No one forced her to smoke; she's responsible for her own actions, so stop acting as if she didn't have anything to do with what happened. You young bitches want to hang out and do everything you're big enough to do, but you can't handle the consequences. I'm tired of you bitches trying to play the part; you don't know anything about this hood life. This is my last time telling you to keep your mouth shut, because if you don't, I'm going to shut it for you."

*Stormi 2: You have to be kidding me, you're really gon' let her talk to you like that. I'm telling you the time is coming when you're going to have to fuck her up and I can't wait, because when you release that **Storm** on her ass it's gon' be all over for her.*

It had been a long night. I was getting ready for bed when my mother entered my room and asked me to sit down. She wanted to talk to me. *I hope she doesn't ask me anything about Shannon.*

"Are you alright Stormi? I know seeing your best friend hanging from the end of a rope can be devastating."

"I'm okay Mom; I never expected this from Shannon."

"What's going on with Shannon?"

"I don't know."

"Yes, you do. You know exactly what's going on. You and Shannon are thick as thieves. Shannon tried to kill herself, and you're going to sit here and tell me that you have no idea why? That's a lie from the pits of hell. We are going to sit here all night until you decide to tell me what's going on."

We sat for an hour before my mother started talking to me again. I knew my mother was mad, but I couldn't tell her what happened. I couldn't bring myself to snitch. My mother explained to me how it was my responsibility to Shannon's family to tell what was going on with Shannon. She sat on the edge of my bed staring at me waiting for me to talk, but I never did. She picked up the phone to call Dominquez Valley Hospital where Shannon was taken.

She spoke with the head nurse who told my mom that Shannon was still unconscious.

"Stormi, I'm going to give you one last time to tell me what's going on or I'm going to ground you for a month."

I just wanted to be a little girl again. This was too much to handle. I couldn't carry this burden; it was getting too heavy.

Stormi 1: It is not your burden to carry, the word of God says, "Cast your burdens on the Lord and He shall sustain you." Tell your mother what is going on. She can help you.

Stormi 2: Don't be a fool. You don't want to be labeled as a snitch. Think before you speak. I don't like your so-called friends and I know that eventually we are going to have to hurt those that hurt you. If you snitch, they are going to beat yo'ass. We are not prepared to handle them yet. Keep your mouth closed.

Finally, my mother decided she was going to bed, but not without having me read Psalms 41:9, "*Even my own familiar friend in whom I trusted, who ate my bread, has lifted up his heel against me.*" I read the scripture, but I didn't quite understand it.

"What does it mean, Mom?"

"The scripture is saying that Shannon is your friend and she trusts you. You have eaten dinner together, shared secrets, everything that best friends do. She lays in the hospital in a coma; she can't tell her story, but you can and you refuse to. You have lifted up your heel against her. What kind of friend are you? You have a good night and I trust things will be clearer to you in the morning."

What the hell, I didn't tell her to smoke. She could have refused just like I did, but now my mom was on my head. What happened? What's going on Stormi? Can she just leave me the hell alone? Stop trying to make me feel guilty.

≈ ≈ ≈

Was it morning already? I didn't get any sleep last night. My heart was heavy. I still didn't know what to do, but I felt the guilt creeping in. I was so close to telling my mother what happened. I was terrified. If I were to tell, it would mess up a lot of people's lives. I didn't see how telling was going to help Shannon. The damage was done. She needed to wake her ass up and tell her own story.

I picked up the phone and called the hospital. I spoke with the head nurse.

"I'm calling to check on Shannon Roberts. Can you tell me how she's doing?"

"Are you a family member?"

"Yes, I'm her sister."

"She's much better today. She's not talking but she's up."

"Praise the Lord! Can she have visitors?"

"No, she's on a seventy-two-hour hold."

"Okay, thank you."

That scripture my mother had me read last night was ringing in my head. Did she really believe that I was not a good friend to Shannon? I thought I was a good friend. If she wanted people to know what happened, she would have left a suicide note. I kept her secret, so I felt like I was a good friend.

The phone rang and it was James.

"How is Shannon doing?"

"I'm not sure, they have her on a seventy-two-hour hold. I believe only her parents get to see her."

James sighed heavily.

"What's wrong with you, James?"

"Nothing, man, she just tripped out, she on some real crazy shit. I wish that bitch had checked out of here. I can't stand a weak bitch!"[1]

"I can't believe you just said that. Life is valuable and you just DISMISSED her like she ain't shit."

"She's weak! If she doesn't want to live, that's on her. I'm just saying you keep putting the blame on King. She didn't have to smoke with him. That was her choice."

"I can't believe you're that cold blooded. Yes, she has to take responsibility for her actions, but she didn't know she was smoking PCP, and she had no intentions of fucking King's black ass."

That conversation made my skin crawl. James was just worried about himself. I was starting to see him as a self-centered bastard. How could he be so insensitive? He couldn't possibly think what King did was okay.

"Look Stormi, I know Shannon is your friend and she's my friend, too. I need you to understand that if it gets out about Shannon and King, many lives are going to be affected, including yours. I'm not only concerned about myself, but I'm also concerned for you. You became an accomplice to the so-called crime when we took her to the motel."

"What?"

"Yes, you're a part of this, so please think before you speak."

They call me Stormi.

Chapter Seven

It was early Monday morning and the phone rings. I picked up the phone, only to hear that my mother had answered it first. It was Reese calling.

"Hello Mrs. Johnson, may I speak with Stormi?"

"I have it, Mom." I waited for my mother to hang up the phone before I began to speak.

"Stormi are you there?"

"Yes, I'm here. What's up, Reese?"

"I see your friend Shannon just made it home this morning. You make sure she doesn't have plans to run her mouth."

"I'm not making sure of nothing. You handle your own shit."

"James told me to tell you to make sure she keeps her mouth closed."

"James doesn't need to send me assignments through you. If he needs me to do something, then he can call and ask me himself. Who do you think you guys are? The mafia! Leave me the fuck alone. If Shannon were going to talk, she would have done so by now. It's obvious she doesn't want anyone to know what happened. She didn't leave a suicide note. You know, Reese, one minute you're my friend and the next minute you're talking shit to me. Just because you're older doesn't give you the right to push me around. I'm getting tired of it. Why don't you fuck with someone your own age? My cousin was just released from Civil Brand. She's your age, and I'm sure she would love to beat yo' ass. Just tell me the time and place and I will make sure she's there."

"Look, Stormi, I'm just doing what needs to be done. You have to respect the neighborhood and once you get older, you will understand how things operate. Call your fuckin' cousin, she not trying to see me. If you want to start a war let's get it started."

"Okay, Reese, let's get it started. You running around here doing the dirty work for King's black ass, all you talk about is this hood code. Well guess what bitch, I'm tired of yo' shit. Do you really think you can handle my cousin? Girl you are in for a rude awakening. Do you remember my cousins that came over on the Fourth of July? Well they are from a gang called Way Down Under (WDU) and they will bury yo' ass "way down under." I want you to keep fuckin' with me, so they can come and fuck you and all the homies up."

"Stormi, this is getting out of hand. It's not that serious. We both need to calm down. I don't want to fight with you, but if I have to, I will. You can call your cousins; you're not the only one with family. I know you don't believe me, but we have to straighten this shit out for everyone's sake, including yours."

I hung up the phone in Reese's face.

Stormi 2: I can't believe you said something to her. It's a first time for everything, but I need you to go a little bit harder the next time. However, I give you your props; you tried. You see, people like Reese need they ass beat.. I'm excited; I know in due time her beat down is gon' take place. She's getting ready to go through the STORM! You can show her better than you can tell her.

After I got off the phone with Reese, I sat on my bed contemplating going to see Shannon. I was nervous. I didn't know what to say to her. I still couldn't believe she tried to take her own life. Her suicide attempt reminded me of a movie I watched.

Stormi 1: This is not the movies, this is real life, you have to go see your friend and talk to her, let her know that God loves her and that life is precious. God is the giver and creator of life; it's a sin to take your own life.

I got up to get dressed.

My little sister Anastasia was sitting on her bed, staring at me. "Stormi, you're so fast, you and your friends… Why would Shannon try to kill herself? I bet it has something to do with what you do on the phone at night."

"Girl, what are you talking about?"

"I hear you on the phone at night Stormi. You think I'm asleep but I'm not. You're nasty and disgusting. I see you touch yourself while you're on the phone talking to

James. You're going to hell. I should tell Mommy about the things you do."

"Shut up Asia!"

I wanted to hit her in her mouth, she's too nosey, and she gets on my nerves. I wished I had my own room. I pushed by her and went into the bathroom to get dressed so I could go and visit Shannon.

≈ ≈ ≈

I knocked on the door. Mrs. Roberts greeted me with a sad look on her face.

"Hello Mrs. Roberts, can Shannon have company?"

Mrs. Roberts's escorted me to Shannon's room. She opened the door; Shannon was sitting on the bed, staring out the window. Mrs. Roberts closed the door. I immediately ran over to hug Shannon. I didn't know what to expect. I was happy that God had given my friend a second chance at life.

Shannon stared at me with glossy eyes and said, in a very demonic voice, "If I was willing to hang myself, you should have had enough respect for me to let me die! It's my right to take away the air that I breathe. If you love me, you would have let me go. You are a selfish witch!"

"Shannon, are you serious! Why would you say something like that? What's going on with you? We are best friends. We tell each other everything. You know I have your back. We could have worked through this. There was no need for you to try to end your life."

"Speak for yourself. King didn't fuck you. I bet you didn't know I was a virgin! I actually wanted to save myself for my husband. You just assumed I was fucking! My world has been turned upside down. You're only a virgin once in this life and that bastard took away my opportunity to choose. How can I live with this? You thought because I didn't talk about it, I didn't remember. I remember every detail, that stinky fucker pushed his black anaconda dick inside of me and fucked me like a ragdoll. He used and abused my body. He fucked me with anger and resentment; he told me as he fucked me that I thought I was too good for anyone in the neighborhood, that I act like my shit don't stink. He said, "Well you gon' learn today. I'm gon' take yo' pussy and make it mine. When I finish with you, you will wish you were dead!"

I was all choked up. I had no idea what to say to Shannon; the words would not come out of my mouth. My best friend was brutally raped. I could never image this happening to someone I loved by someone I knew. King had taken her will to live on purpose; he set out to make her want to kill herself.

He succeeded in killing her spirit. How could I help my friend fight for her life? What could I say to make this better? Nothing! I just held her tight. Shannon's mother walked into the room to let me know the visit was over; it was time for Shannon to take her medicine.

I kissed Shannon goodbye on her forehead. Shannon stared at me with the same blank stare she had when King raped her. Her mother told me I could visit her tomorrow.

When I got home, the first person I saw was my mother. I wanted to fall into her arms and cry, but I couldn't. I wanted to tell her how King had hurt Shannon, but I couldn't share that either. I wanted to tell her I understood the scripture, but what would have been the point?

Shannon was alive and if she wanted her story told, she was going to have to be the one to tell it.

I went to my room and climbed into my bed. I was thinking about all the events that had taken place over the last couple of months. It made me sad. I pulled the cover over my head; I didn't want to see the beautiful sunlight shining through the window. I wanted to be in the dark. That's how I felt, very dark! My youngest sister, Valencia, came into the room and sat on my bed.

"What's wrong Stormi? Why do you have the cover over your head?"

"Nothing's wrong, I'm okay."

"You seem sad. Is it because of what happened to Shannon? I prayed for her the night she went to the hospital. You have to trust God. She is going to be okay. Where's your faith?"

I pulled the cover from over my head and looked at my sister's innocent face. I sat up in the bed and gave her a hug. Tears rolled down my face, and all I could think about was if it happened to Shannon, it could happen to any one of us, even my little sisters. I was sure this was not the first time King raped somebody, and I was sure it wouldn't be the last.

⋍ ⋍ ⋍

Several weeks had gone by. I visited Shannon every day and she appeared to be getting stronger mentally. We watched movies, played games, went to the mall — all the things we did before the rape. Shannon had not once mentioned King's name nor had I. I didn't want her to have a setback. In fact, I hadn't seen King, Reese, or James for quite some time now. With all the time I had been spending with Shannon, I actually hadn't missed James. We had talked on the phone, but the conversations were brief. I still loved him, but I loved my girl Shannon too, and right now, she needed me. James was on the backburner for now.

The doorbell rang. I was not expecting anyone. I was in my room watching TV and painting my nails, and in walked Joyce. I was pleasantly surprised. I hadn't seen her in a while.

"Hey Miss Stormi, how are you? Long time no see."

"Hey Joyce." We embraced. "Where have you been hiding?"

"My mother made me stay at home; she didn't want me to visit with Shannon. She thinks Shannon is a bad influence."

"What are you talking about?" I exclaimed. "Does she think Shannon is going to influence you to commit suicide?"

"Girl, no, she thinks she might influence me to have sex. You know how my mother is; all my sisters have illegitimate kids and more than one baby daddy. I'm the youngest girl; she's trying to preserve my jewel box." Joyce laughed loudly.

"Who told your mother Shannon had sex?"

"My mother overheard my brother and his friends talking about Shannon, they said, 'Shannon had sex with King, and that she was upset because King didn't want to be in a relationship with her; she couldn't image having sex with him and they not be together'."

"So tell me Stormi, did Shannon get dick whipped or what?"

Joyce is laughing her ass off. I was looking at her wondering if she was serious.

I couldn't believe she just asked me that. The next thing I knew, my hands were around her throat. I choked that bitch until she fell on the floor gasping for air.

"What's wrong with you? Why are you acting crazy! I can't believe you just choked me."

"Believe it, bitch! You're lucky you're still breathing."

"Damn Stormi, you didn't have to go to that extreme. I was just playing around. I don't have control of what they are saying about Shannon. That's the word in the streets."

"Joyce, what the hell is wrong with you! Bitch, you came down here to be nosey. You're not the least bit concerned about Shannon. You want to gossip about someone that we have been friends with since we were in elementary school. She has always been a good friend to all of us. You have no sense of loyalty. I can't believe you! Did you really think I was going to sit and talk about my best friend with you? King raped Shannon bitch! When you confided in us about your cousin rubbing on you while you were sleeping, we never sat up and talked about your cousin's incestuous ass. We put ourselves in harm's way to help you. It was Shannon and I hiding in the closet waiting for your cousin to come into your room in the middle of the night. When he crawled into bed with you, Shannon and I jumped out of the closet with the camera and took his picture. He has never ever entered your room again. You have a lot of nerve, you ungrateful bitch. How soon we forget who our friends are. If the right people found out about what your cousin was doing, he would be in jail."

"I'm so sorry Stormi; it wasn't my idea to do this. My sister Jackie made me do it. You know how messy my sister is, she wouldn't stop harassing me about it. I feel so bad about this."

"You should feel bad! You could have told me what was going on, and we could have come up with something to tell your sister! We all have some type of dysfunction in our family, but your family takes the cake. Your sister is nosey as fuck! She sent your dumbass down here to get information from me, and you really thought I was going to fall for that. Ask her about Reese's daddy."

"What are you talking about Stormi?"

"Your sister has been fucking Reese's daddy for several months. She fucked Lisa's daddy, too. Your sister is the biggest hoe on the block. Just the other day I saw her in the car giving Reese's daddy a blowjob!"

"Don't lie on my sister, Stormi."

"Girl, I don't have to lie, you know your sister is a hoe. She has two babies and she's talking about she doesn't know who the daddy is, that's a lie."

"Stormi, she knows the father of her children. She just lied about not knowing so that she can get a county check."

"Bitch, please, one of those babies I know for sure is Lisa's daddy's baby. Why do you think they moved? Yes, he got a new job, but Lisa's mom found out and threatened to leave him so he changed jobs and moved out of the state. Your sister is a home wrecker and a tramp. So, the next time you need something to talk about, ask your sister who's her baby daddy!"

Joyce walked out of my room, and I was right behind her. She got to the front door, turned around and looked at me with tears rolling down her face. I opened the door and pushed her ass out.

They call me Stormi.

Chapter Eight

It was quiet in the neighborhood. I hadn't seen anyone lately. I hadn't told Shannon about the incident with Joyce. I didn't think it was worth mentioning; Shannon had enough on her plate. She had been doing so well. I figured I'd keep it to myself, as there was no need to give her anything else to cause her worry.

It's odd, but I hadn't spoken with James in days. I knew I wasn't allowed over his house without talking to him first, but when I called, no one answered the phone. I decided to go to his house and pay him a visit anyway. I rang the doorbell, but no one answered the door. James' car was in the driveway, so I continued ringing the bell.

After ringing the bell for five minutes, I decided to leave. As I was leaving, James' mother pulled into the driveway.

"Hello Stormi, are you looking for James? He should be in his room. He never hears the doorbell. You can go in, he might be asleep."

I entered the house and proceeded to James' room. I knocked on his bedroom door.

"Who is it?"

"It's me Stormi; your mother let me in."

"Give me a minute; I have to put some clothes on."

"I've seen your goods before."

"Girl, don't come over here disrespecting my mother's house."

"I'm just kidding."

While waiting for James to get dressed, it sounded like someone was in the room with him. I pressed my ear to the door, but I couldn't make out what they were saying. I knew I wasn't crazy, I heard people talking in his room.

James finally opened the door and led me straight to the living room.

"What's up Stormi, why are you here?"

"It sounded like you were talking to someone. Is someone in your room?"

James ignored my question, and continued to ask why I was at his house.

"I wanted to talk to you about what's being said about Shannon, and the fact that I haven't seen you in a while is another issue."

"Okay, we'll talk later. I will call you in about an hour or two."

"Don't call too late; you know I have a curfew."

"If I know anything, it's that!"

As I was walking home, the thought of someone being in his room crossed my mind again. I know I wasn't hearing things.

Stormi 2: Of course, you heard someone in his room. He's a liar; someone was in his room. Trust your gut feelings, turn around, and go back. Hide across the street. I'm sure you will see someone leaving his house.

I just didn't feel like playing investigator, so I went home. I was tired; I could use a nap. On my way home, I saw Joyce's sister, Jackie, sitting on the porch. I had to pass her to get to my house. I didn't know if Joyce told her what happened, but I guess I would soon find out.

Jackie was smoking a cigarette and drinking a Coke.

"Hey Stormi, how are you doing? I haven't seen you walking around here lately."

"I'm good. I've been busy."

"Girl, that's what I hear. They tell me you've been taking good care of Shannon. How is that going?"

"I don't know what you're talking about; Shannon doesn't need me to take care of her. She's great!"

"If she's so great, why did she try to kill herself?"

"Jackie, you should express your concerns to her. I'm sure she can answer any questions you may have. I don't understand why everyone asks me how she's doing. Why don't you go and visit her and then you can judge for yourself."

"It's not that serious, you're with her all the time that's why I asked you."

"She's not only my friend; she is your friend as well. So why don't you take some time out to go see her?"

"Stormi, I asked you a simple question and you're making a big deal out of nothing."

"I will talk to you later, Jackie. I will tell Shannon you asked about her."

"Thanks, Stormi. Tell her I'm praying for her."

"Yeah, I bet you are."

She doesn't give two cents about what happens to Shannon.

I continued on my way home, I saw Shannon's mother outside washing her car.

"Hello Mrs. Roberts, how are you?"

"I'm fine Stormi. What are you up to?"

"Nothing much, where's Shannon?"

"She's sleep; she has been extremely tired lately."

"Okay, I'll give her a call later."

Finally, I got into my bed. I lie down and close my eyes. I could use about an hour of sleep. James would be calling in about an hour.

I awake to my brother, Derrick, pushing me.

"What?"

"Girl, James is outside looking for you. He told me to come get you."

"Okay."

I washed my face and brushed my teeth before talking to James.

It was too late for me to leave the house, so I was going to have to talk to James on the porch. I told Derrick to come outside with me just in case my parents saw James they wouldn't think anything of it if Derrick were outside, too.

I was greeted with a hug from James.

"What's going on, Stormi?"

"James, I want to know what the word on the street is about Shannon. I got a visit from Joyce and she tells me people are talking about how she flipped out because King didn't want to be with her. Jackie sent Joyce to my house to get information from me."

"Stormi, don't worry about what's been said, you can't control what people say. You know Jackie is nosey; she needs something to talk about. No one is focusing on Shannon anymore; things have been quiet. It's all good in the hood! So don't worry your little head about rumors. That's all they are."

"Well, okay James, if you say so."

Derrick walked up. "Stormi, I'm going in the house. You need to come on."

James kissed me on my forehead and he leaves.

⧐ ⧐ ⧐

It was the next morning, and I had slept in my clothes. I must have been extremely tired; I couldn't believe no one woke me. I got up to go to the bathroom and in walks Valencia into the room.

"Sleepy head, you're finally up. We tried to wake you last night, but you wouldn't move, so Mom told us to leave you alone and just let you sleep, and you slept through the night. You never said a word..."

"I guess I got some much-needed rest." I looked out my bedroom window. The sun was shining brightly. I felt so rejuvenated. Today was going to be a nice day. I got dressed and went into the kitchen to get some cereal. Anastasia and Valencia were watching cartoons. I asked them if they wanted to go to the park, and without hesitation, I got a big yes!

I asked my mom if I could drive the station wagon, so we didn't have to walk. My mother handed over the keys and we were on our way. We arrived at the park; we spread the blanket on the ground, and set up the lunch my mother had prepared. I sat on the blanket and watched Asia and Valencia run to the swings.

I just wanted to lie down, close my eyes, and enjoy the heat from the sun. I made sure to tell Asia that she was in charge, and not to leave out of the area. The sun felt so good on my body. I felt myself drifting off, almost asleep. I needed to relax, no worries just peace. *Shannon should have come with us*, I thought, but I hadn't spent any time with my sisters so today was sister day.

I had only closed my eyes for ten minutes and when I opened them I found Kings black dirty ass at the swings, talking to my sisters. *What the fuck!* I jumped up in a panic and I ran over to them.

"Hello Stormi. I haven't seen you in a while. I was just checking to see if your sisters wanted some ice cream from the ice cream truck."

"King, they're fine. They don't need anything. I can get them whatever they need."

I stared so hard at him; I could have burned a hole in his head. I tried to keep my composure. If I were to get crazy, Asia would definitely tell my mother and I didn't need that!

"Stormi, I'm like the neighborhood watch. I'll make sure nothing happens to them. Your sisters sure are pretty."

"The last time you watched someone she ended up raped! There is no need for you to watch my sisters."

"Stormi, you're going to have to stop spreading that lie about me. You have people scared to talk to me. I didn't rape anyone."

"You're a liar! Get the Fuck! Away from my sisters."

King walked away, shaking his head.

I told Asia and Valencia not to accept anything from anybody. "I don't care if they are from our neighborhood," I reiterated.

I walked back to the blanket and sat down, I was too nervous to lie back down. I had to make sure I kept a close eye on my sisters. The park was busy. It appeared everyone had the same idea—to come out and enjoy the sun. I looked over at the basketball court; I saw ten very handsome, shirtless guys playing ball. They looked like professional players, but I knew better than that. I didn't recognize anyone playing.

People were gathering around to watch the game. It's a good game. This one guy is giving them the blues; he's dunking on their heads. He has to be six-feet-five; he's tall and super fine and I can't take my eyes off him.

Swoosh! He made another basket. All net baby. This guy is good. He was flying in the air like a bird. They gave him the ball again, he goes for the layup; slammed the ball in the net, but when he came down, he landed hard on his ankle, which took him out of the game.

He limped over to the sideline. He caught me staring at him and gave me a nod and a smile as if to say hello. He was much older…probably a college guy. He was nursing his ankle; he took an ace bandage out of his bag and wrapped his ankle. His team was struggling without him, but they pulled it off and won the game. They gave each other high fives and prepared to leave the court. He was limping in my direction. The closer he got to me, the more I tried to make myself noticeable.

I sat upright with a slight arch in my back to make my tits appear bigger. This dude was handsome; he had a nice smile and nice teeth, and hazel eyes. I tried to play it cool and appear to be older than I am.

"Hello, how are you?" he asked me.

"I'm good. How are you?"

"I was fine until I landed on my ankle. I have to go home and ice it. My name is Bryce, what's yours?"

"My name is Stormi."

He gave me a big smile and repeated my name. "Stormi…that's different."

"That's because I'm different."

He smiled. "It was nice meeting you Stormi; hopefully I will see you again."

"Hopefully!" I replied.

 He smiled and walked away.

They call me Stormi.

Chapter Nine

𝓨esterday was a good day! I spent time with my sisters and relaxed. That Bryce sure was cute. I couldn't wait to tell Shannon about him. *Wow, the fact that I was even thinking about someone else was different for me.*

I called Shannon; I hadn't spoken with her in days. The phone rang a few times before she answered.

"Hello."

"Hello, Shannon?"

"Stormi, how are you?"

"I'm good; we haven't spoken to each other in a while, so I thought I would give you a call. What have you been up to?"

"I've been sleeping a lot. I'm so tired; I don't have any energy. My mother said I need some vitamins. Stormi I haven't had a period for a month. I feel like my period is trying to start; my breasts are tender and I feel bloated, but my body is just going through the motions."

As I was listening to her describe her symptoms, the first thing that came to mind was that she might be pregnant. I listened to her go on and on about how sick she felt.

"Shannon I think you should take a pregnancy test."

There was silence on the phone.

"Hello? Shannon, did you hear me?"

"Yes Stormi, I heard what you said. Oh my God, that couldn't be possible!"

"Yes Shannon, it could be possible. Do not panic; we just need to rule it out. We can go to the free clinic and you can take a pregnancy test."

"I can't believe I have to take a pregnancy test; what am I going to do if it's positive?"

"Don't worry about that; there's a good chance that you're not. Get dressed and we will walk to the clinic."

"Stormi, everyone knows my parents. I can't walk into a free clinic and take a pregnancy test. Someone just might tell them."

"You're right; we need someone else to do it for you. I'll get Joyce to do it. She already knows that I had sex with James. She will do it for me with no problem. I need you to pee in a cup, but it has to have a top on it. I'm coming to pick it up. You don't even have to go to the clinic."

"Thanks so much Stormi, I really appreciate you."

I picked up Shannon's urine sample and headed to Joyce's house. I didn't even call her to let her know that I was coming. I got to Joyce's house and I rang the doorbell.

"Who's there?"

"It's Stormi. I'm looking for Joyce."

The door opened and Joyce peeked out. "Hello, Stormi."

"Hey, Joyce, I need you to go to the free clinic with me."

Joyce looked very shocked. "You want me to go to the free clinic with you?"

"That's what I said."

"Okay, let me change my shoes and I will be right out."

I sat on her steps and waited for her. She came out and we walked to the clinic.

"Stormi, does this mean we are still friends?"

"Yes, we're still friends, but if you ever betray Shannon or me, you will pay for it."

"Stormi, you know I'm so sorry for what I did. It won't happen again. Why are we going to the free clinic?"

"I need you to take a pregnancy test for me. If I take it, someone may tell my mother, but if you take it, no one will care. It's expected because all your sisters had babies early."

"Okay, Stormi, whatever you need me to do, but how will I take the test for you?"

"I peed in a cup already; all you have to do is pour my pee in your cup and let them test it. They will think it's your pee."

"Okay, Stormi."

Once we arrived at the clinic, a nurse handed Joyce a sterile container and told her she needed a urine sample. Joyce goes into the bathroom and faked peeing in the container. She poured Shannon's pee into the container the nurse had given her. Joyce took the urine sample to the lab and returned back to the nurse's desk. The nurse handed Joyce a card.

"Call back in an hour. The person that answers the phone will ask for your code. The code number is 593. Once they verify your code, they will tell you if your test is positive or negative."

Joyce and I walked back to her house. We sat and talked for more than an hour before I headed back to Shannon's house. Once I arrived back at Shannon's house, I handed her the card with the free clinic's phone number and the code. I waited patiently as she made the call. I was sure the test would be ready. She slammed the phone down suddenly, and ran into the bathroom.

I knocked on the bathroom door. "Shannon, can I come in?"

"Yes Stormi."

I entered the bathroom and Shannon was sitting on the toilet. She had tears running down her face. My heart ached for her.

"It's positive!" she shouted

I looked at Shannon and I walked over to her and held her tight.

"It's going to be okay Shannon. We can make it through this. Let's go back to your room."

Shannon sat on her bed, looking out the window. I hesitated to speak, but someone had to say something.

"Okay Shannon, what do you want to do?"

"Stormi, I can't have a baby, I'm not ready for that. I have to get rid of it. There's no way I'm going to have King's baby."

"What do you mean get rid of it? You want to have an abortion?"

"Yes, I want an abortion. I'm not bringing a baby into this world. This baby is the result of a rape."

"Well, you have to tell your mother what's going on so she can help you."

"My intentions are to not tell my mother anything. You and I will handle this. We will take the bus to Long Beach to the clinic."

"Shannon, this is too much for me. We need help. We need to tell an adult what's going on. I'm not risking it this time."

"My mother is going to have a heart attack if I tell her I'm pregnant. Should I tell her I was raped, too?"

"You tell her whatever you want. I will stand behind you one hundred percent."

"Stormi, I don't want my mother to know King raped me."

"Okay, then tell her you made a mistake and got drunk at the party and you think someone put something in your drink. Tell her you don't remember what happened that way she would understand why you tried to commit suicide."

"You're right; I think that will work. I'm so scared Stormi, I don't want my mother to hate me."

"She won't hate you, Shannon. Your mother loves you and she will take care of you. That's what mothers are for, just trust her."

A peace came over Shannon. I hugged her and told her she was going to be okay.

As I was getting ready to leave, Shannon grabbed my hand. "Stormi, I want you to go with me and my mother to take care of this."

"Shannon, if your mother is okay with me going I will, but you know that means I would have to tell my mother what's going on, so think about it and if you still want me to go, I will get permission from my mother. Call me later."

I left Shannon's house and walked across the street to go home.

☙ ☙ ☙

Days passed and I hadn't heard a word from Shannon. I was starting to get worried. I was trying to give her some space, but the last time I gave her space, she hung herself.

This had been a drama-filled summer. I didn't have any fun; I was actually ready to go back to school. I turned fourteen and I didn't have a party. James didn't give me a gift. My best friend tried to kill herself and now she was pregnant. I had sex for the first time and I regretted it. Joyce, my childhood friend, turned against Shannon and me. Reese's crazy ass threatened me. I found out if you break the hood code, you would get your ass beat. What a summer!

I was getting ready to call Shannon when my mother walked into the room.

"I need to talk to you Stormi."

My mother had that "I'm serious" look on her face, so I sat down to listen to what she had to say.

"I spoke with Shannon's mother and apparently Shannon is pregnant. She is going to have an abortion and insists on you being there. "Stormi what's going on?"

"Didn't Shannon's mother tell you?"

"Yes, she did, but I would like to hear what you have to say."

"Mom, what do you want me to say? My best friend is pregnant and she wants to have an abortion. She believes someone put something in her drink. She has no memory of who she had sex with, and that is why she tried to kill herself. Before all of this happened she was a virgin and she wanted to save herself for marriage."

"Stormi, Shannon's mother is beside herself. She doesn't believe Shannon is telling her everything."

"Mom, Shannon told me the same story. I wasn't with her when it happened. I'm just trying to support her. She doesn't want to have a baby and she needs her mom's support. I would feel the same way if it was me. We have to be there for her. That's what counts!"

"I understand Stormi, but this needs to be reported and there needs to be an investigation."

"Mom! What are you talking about? You're taking things too far. She doesn't want an investigation; she just wants to move on with her life. This is exactly why we don't talk to our parents; you just don't get it. Please don't start putting all this investigation stuff in her mom's head. Let it go."

"Well Stormi, I don't know how I feel about you going to an abortion clinic. I don't believe in abortion and I don't think you should go. Abortion is against my religion."

"Mom! Are you serious? She's my best friend and I need to be there for her. This has nothing to do with me. You just don't get it."

"Stormi, you're my daughter and I have to do what I think is best for you."

"What's best for me? You want to make this about me. Okay, if I was the one pregnant, your religion would have nothing to do with it. There's no way daddy would let me bring a bastard child into this house at fourteen, and you know it. You already have six children. You would not raise your daughter's bastard child. You would be taking me to the clinic just like Shannon's mother is taking her. No disrespect mom, but it's easy to say what you would do until something happens to you and you have to rethink what you believe. I will be going to support Shannon. I talked her into telling her mom. She wanted me to ride the bus with her to the clinic to have the procedure done. I told her she needed to tell her mother what was going on."

My mother sat quietly. I didn't know if she was contemplating knocking the shit out of me, or what.

"Stormi, you are growing up very quickly, and you make some very good points. If you are determined to go, I won't stop you, but I put my trust in God. He is the head of my life and I will continue to pray for Shannon and her family. You are just a little girl and you have no idea what I would do in the same situation. The God I serve is an awesome God and I pray to Him daily to cover my children with His Blood! I trust God!"

I hugged my mother very tight. I was no longer the little girl she thought I was. I loved my mother. I would hate for her to know that I was no longer a virgin. It would have broken her heart if she knew about the dirty mattress ordeal or the backseat of the car. How I wished I had done things differently.

$$\sim \sim \sim$$

It was seven o'clock the next morning, and we had to be at the clinic by eight o'clock. I was riding in the back seat of Mrs. Robert's car. I closed my eyes and said a prayer. I was extremely nervous. "Father God, in the name of Jesus, please keep my friend safe."

We arrived at the clinic. Shannon and I walked in holding hands. Tears welled up in her eyes. I knew she wanted to cry, but she was holding back her tears.

We sat down and waited for Shannon's name to be called.

Shannon whispered in my ear. "If I don't make it, I just want you to know that I love you and I appreciate you being here for me."

Instantly, tears ran down my face. I grabbed her so tightly, and whispered to her, "I will see you in a couple of hours."

The nurse came to the door to get Shannon and escorted her back. Mrs. Roberts kissed Shannon on the forehead and I blew her a kiss.

My stomach was in knots. I looked over at Mrs. Roberts. She looked so worried. I sat next to her and held her hand. They told us our total wait time would be at least two hours. I thought about the conversation I had with my mother, and all I could hear her say was, "I trust God, I trust God!" I got up and walked around, and "I trust God" was ringing in my head. I couldn't think of anything else. I found myself saying, "I trust God, I trust God." Mrs. Roberts asked me if I was okay. I acknowledged her with a nod and a smile.

The nurse came to the door and called Mrs. Roberts' name. I got nervous; it had only been thirty minutes. There was no way they could be finished. The nurse was taking Mrs. Roberts to the back. Mrs. Roberts gestured for me to come with her.

The nurse didn't say a word other than, "Please follow me."

We entered the doctor's office, who was seated behind his desk. Shannon's mother was very upset and started to shout, "Oh my God, what has happened to my daughter?" She fell to her knees.

I kept repeating, "I trust God, I trust God."

The doctor jumped up and I helped Mrs. Roberts to a chair.

"Mrs. Roberts, calm down," the doctor said. "All is well with your daughter! We didn't perform the surgery. We put your daughter to sleep and before we could get started, she woke up. We administered a higher dose of anesthesia and she went back to sleep. We started the procedure and she woke up again. She said that the Lord spoke to her and told her to keep her baby. We administered another dose of anesthesia and she would not go back to sleep. In all my years of practice, I have never experienced anything like this. We can't perform this procedure on your daughter. The anesthesia, for some reason, will not work on her."

All I could think of was *I trust God.* I couldn't wait to tell my mother, I could only wish to have the faith that she has!

We were escorted to Shannon's room. She was up putting her clothes on. As soon as she saw us, she said, "I'm having my baby. The Lord showed me that my child is a blessing from God and that I have to let the baby come forth. He told me not to worry about the father that He will be the father to my child and that He will provide for us. I have never experienced anything like this in my life, but I do believe it was God speaking to me."

Mrs. Roberts looked at Shannon, and said, "To God be the Glory."

They call me Stormi.

Chapter Ten

Shannon was doing very well. She moved to Arkansas with her mom's sister where she would have the baby. The summer was ending and it was time to get ready for school. My mother decided to send my siblings and me to a different school. With all that has gone on, she thought we needed a new environment.

I was all for going to a new school. My best friend was gone, so I was open for change. I spoke to Shannon once a week. She sounded so happy. I didn't understand what had happened with her, but I don't question God. My mother was so excited for Shannon, she said, "God showed up and showed out." She was actually going to let me go to Arkansas when it was time for Shannon to have the baby.

I had two weeks left before I returned to school. It was quiet on the block. I would see Reese in passing; Joyce and I were working on our friendship. I would see King hanging out at the liquor store, and James and I were still a couple.

Everyone was curious as to why Shannon left. I received several phone calls in regards to Shannon. Reese was the main one calling. I didn't give her any info. I advised her to call Shannon's mother if she were so concerned about her.

I had to admit, it felt like the days went by much slower since Shannon left. I really didn't have much to do.

It was a hot day. I wanted to go and get some ice cream. I called Joyce to see if she wanted to walk to Thrifty's drug store.

"Hey, Joyce, I'm on my way to Thrifty's to get ice cream. Would you like to go with me?"

"Hey, Stormi, girl, I'm burning up over here. I definitely want ice cream."

"Okay, I should be at your door in ten minutes."

I asked Anastasia and Valencia if they wanted to go with me. Of course, they did. We arrived at Joyce's house and she was sitting on her porch waiting for us.

"Hello Anastasia, hello Valencia how are you all doing today?"

Anastasia waved at Joyce and Valencia just smiled.

"Joyce, it's so hot I think we will fill up our portable pool in the backyard and play in the water. You're invited to cool off at our house."

"That sounds like fun, Stormi."

We got our ice cream and headed back home. We had to pass James' street on our way. I looked down his street and saw James and Reese leaning against her car talking. I did a double take. Reese was standing between James' legs, her arms were wrapped around his neck, and she was kissing him.

I dropped my cone on the ground. Joyce, seeing what I was seeing, told me to keep walking.

I started running toward James' house.

Joyce was screaming, "Stormi! Stormi, what are you doing?"

She ran after me, my sisters were screaming and running after me, too. When I ran up on James, he was just standing there, looking at me.

Reese yelled, "Tell her James! Tell this little girl you don't want her ass. Tell her that you just played with her to get the pussy"

James didn't say a word.

Reese walked up to me.

"Take your dumbass home. James doesn't want you; he used you and you fell for it. He's with me. I'm a real woman."

"Go home, Stormi. I'll call you later," James shouted.

Reese was standing there with her hands on her hips, smiling at me.

I was hurt. I didn't know what to do. I was mad! I pushed Reese as hard as I could, and she fell on the grass. I jumped on top of her and struck her in her face. I pulled her short ass hair as hard as I could. She pushed me off her. I struggled, trying to stay on top, but she was too strong. She got on her feet and put her hands up to box me.

My sisters were crying.

We were going in circles, trying to hit each other. I looked at her and said, "I don't want to fight anymore," and began to walk away. As soon as I could see her guard was down, I rushed her and knocked her down. She hit the ground and I tried to knock her head off. My little sisters ran over and started kicking her. She was screaming for help. James ran over and pulled me off her. My sister, Anastasia, kicked her one more time.

James helped Reese get up and took her into his house. I was so mad; I picked up a big ass rock and threw it through his mother's front glass window.

Joyce walked up to me. "Take your sister's home, Stormi. I will take the blame for the window. You have always had my back. Allow me to do this for you!"

They call me Stormi.

Chapter Eleven

❧

Stormi 2: It has been a fucked up summer. Your so-called man is fucking Reese's tramp ass, your best friend was raped, and she tried to kill herself. Now she is pregnant by her rapist. You lost your virginity to a fucked up dude. Your church friends, Chloe and Brandy, turned Sunday school out, and let's not forget Joyce's trifling ass. As we move forward, I suggest that you listen to me. I will never steer you wrong. Make sure you keep that dude Trent's number; you may need him one day.

I was depressed, and I had no one to talk to. My best friend Shannon was in Arkansas dealing with her pregnancy and, even though Joyce took the blame for the broken window, I still didn't think I could trust her. Reese and James rode up and down the street with each other, they have no regard for my feelings. I cried myself to sleep every night.

Stormi 1: Pull yourself together. You have gone through a lot, but God has been with you all the time. Things could have been worse. Soon, you will be attending a new school. That's an opportunity for new friends and new beginnings.

I had three weeks left before I started school. I was so bored, so I walked to the park. I needed time to think. I sat on the swing and started swinging. I swung higher and higher. I was having fun by myself.

Suddenly, I felt someone pushing me. I tried to turn around to see who it was, but they kept dodging me.

"Hey Stormi, how are you?"

I knew the voice, but I couldn't think of his name.

"You forgot about me already, Stormi?"

"No, I know exactly who you are, Bryce!"

Bryce walked directly in front of the swing, so I stopped swinging.

"Bryce what brings you to the park?"

"I came to shoot some hoops. Are you here alone?"

"Yes, I just needed some alone time."

"I can understand that. Come shoot hoops with me. It will take your mind off whatever you're going through."

I got off of the swing and walked over to the basketball court. Bryce gave me the ball. I shoot and I make a basket. We were running around on the court, having fun. I didn't want to get too sweaty, so I told Bryce we needed to take a break. We sat on the park bench.

We talked for hours about our lives and the things we had been through, Bryce lost his mother at birth and his aunt raised him. I discussed with him the relationship I had with James, and how he ended up with Reese. He talked about returning to college and asked me the name of the college I would be attending. I totally avoided the question. It was time for me to go home when Bryce asked for my number. I asked him to give me his instead. He gave me his number and he made me promise to call him. I started walking home and Bryce pulled up alongside me in his car.

"Hey! Stormi, let me take you home."

"I can walk. I don't get in cars with strangers."

"Girl, I'm no stranger. Here, I'll let you hold my driver's license. Get in the car. I had a nice time talking with you. I can at least take you home."

"Well, okay."

What was I thinking getting into his car? I wasn't worried about him doing anything. I was worried about who might see me in the car with him. We got to my street and I could see that my parents weren't home, so I risked letting him drop me off at my house. I hurried out of the car and thanked him for the ride.

The next day, I was standing in the front yard, watering the grass, and Bryce drove down my block. He didn't stop, but he smiled at me and kept going. I wasn't sure what that was about, but I was going to call him and find out. I had to keep him under control, he had no idea that I was fourteen. For some reason, he thought I was in college.

Stormi 2: Make sure you are fucking with the right man this time. My hit list is getting bigger. I'm putting a plan together for all those who have fucked you over. They are going to regret ever doing you wrong. This Bryce dude appears to be cool. Keep your guard up, do not let him into your world too soon, and please don't fall head over heels for this dude. You have to learn from your mistakes.

I waited about an hour before I called Bryce.

"Hello, may I speak with Bryce?"

"This is Bryce, Stormi."

"Why did you drive down my street?"

"You didn't give me your number to call you, so I took the chance of driving down your street to see if I would see you. I enjoyed being with you yesterday and I thought you were going to call me last night."

"I told you I was going to call you."

"Yeah, but you didn't."

"I was taking my time; I didn't want to appear too anxious."

Bryce laughed. "Well, Stormi, it appears I'm the anxious one. I couldn't wait to see you. Let's get together today."

"I have errands to run for my mother, maybe I could meet you at your house."

"That's cool Stormi, what time?"

"I should be there about two o'clock. Let me have your address."

"It's 1934 West Billings Drive." Bryce gave me his address and I got excited. I wouldn't be making the same mistake with him that I had made with James. I would stay in complete control of this situation.

I finished my errands and was on my way to Bryce's house. I pulled up in my mother's station wagon. Bryce was sitting on the front porch waiting on me. Before I could get out the car, he was opening the door for me. *Wow, I feel important.* I looked into his hazel eyes and I just wanted to melt, but I had to remember to remain in control. Bryce escorted me to a back house where he lived. He had his own little hide away. He opened the door for me. He had a small couch, a bed, and a small kitchen all in the same room. I sat on the couch and he turned on the TV. I had maybe two hours before I had to go home. We sat and watched TV and talked about everything under the sun. I found myself laying my head in his lap. He was so easy to talk to, and damn, he was fine. My shirt rose up above my belly button and Bryce took notice. He ran his finger down the hairline on my belly. I tried not to act shy.

"Stormi, I think your hairline on your stomach is sexy."

My heart was beating fast. I looked into his eyes and he leaned in to kiss me. That was the most sensual kiss I had ever had. He inserted his tongue deep in my mouth, we kissed and kissed. He began rubbing all over my body. I started to feel wet between my thighs!

Stormi 2: Don't you dare fuck him on the first date. Get your ass up, and go home. Leave him wanting for more; remain in control and don't give him your number.

What I was feeling had to be nothing but lust. James never kissed me like that; I never felt any wetness between my thighs when we kissed. James was good looking, but Bryce was fine with a capital "F." That was the first time my body was saying "Yes!"

I got on top of Bryce, grinding up and down on him; I felt his pole of life getting hard. We had our clothes on. I didn't intend on taking mine off, but he could take his off if he wanted. I was having a good time grinding on him. I got a major nut and my panties were soaked. I felt so good. *I had better control myself before his pole of life finds its way inside of me.* I stroked his pole. I just wanted to see what it felt like. It was very large. I had no idea what had come over me. I had never been that aggressive. I was not an expert on pole sizes, but I was sure he was packing. The next time I give up the jewel box it would be on my terms.

Stormi 2: Stop acting like a hoe, you barely know him. You have all the time in the world to screw, slow your roll.

Stormi 1: You have just come out of a bad relationship, you lost your virginity and you have committed a major sin. Stop and think before you do things. Consider God's Word in everything.

"I have to go," I said.

He got up and got me some water, and told me he would see me soon. I was so shocked he didn't even try to get my jewel box. He just let me enjoy myself. He walked me to my car and opened the door for me. He leaned in the car and kissed me on the cheek.

Now, he's a gentlemen! James would have screwed me and sent me on my way.

As I drove to the house, all I could think about was Bryce. He was such a nice guy. I wanted to tell him my age, but I feared he wouldn't talk to me anymore. I hated to lie, but I was feeling him and I knew if I told him the truth he wasn't going to mess with me.

Stormi 2:Don't tell him anything. Leave it as it is, he's not going to be your boyfriend. He's going back to college. Live in the moment.

Stormi 1: You should always tell the truth; one lie leads to another. Honesty is the best policy. It will save you grief in the end.

For now, I was going to leave everything the way it was. I was not going to tell Bryce.

I needed to talk to my best friend. My mother let me call Shannon every other week and it was that time. I dialed Shannon's number.

"Hello Shannon, is that you girl? How are you?"

"Stormi, I'm doing well. What's going on in the C-town?"

"Girl not a lot, I'm getting ready for school in a couple of weeks. Have you enrolled in school yet?"

"Girl, I will be attending a school for pregnant girls. I'm looking forward to meeting new people. So far my pregnancy has been easy, no morning sickness."

"That's good, Shannon. I'm glad you're doing well. By the way, I met this new guy. His name is Bryce. He is so fine, Shannon. I can hardly breathe."

"What, Stormi, you are finally over James? I can't believe it."

"I can't believe it either, but spending time with Bryce makes me forget all about James. Bryce is a nice guy, but the thing is, Shannon, he thinks I'm going to college when school starts."

"Stormi, you should not start a relationship built on lies. You know better than that."

"I know Shannon, but it's not like we are going to be in a relationship. He will be leaving for school in a couple of weeks and I'm sure I will never see him again."

"I understand Stormi, but you shouldn't take away his right to choose. He has the right to know that you're a minor. Don't be like King; he took away my right to choose if I wanted to have sex with him."

"Dang Shannon, you make it sound so horrible."

"It is horrible when you put your trust into someone and they disappoint you. The same way James did you; he was messing around with Reese and you at the same time. Don't forget how hurt you felt."

"Okay Shannon, I guess you're right. I will tell him my age the next time I see him. Well, I'm glad that everything is going okay for you. I'll wait to hear from you in two weeks. It will be your turn to call me."

"Okay Stormi, I'll talk to you soon."

Dang, I wish I hadn't even called her. Now I feel super guilty about not telling Bryce my age. I didn't need anything extra to think about, but I couldn't ignore the fact that Shannon was right.

They call me Stormi.

Chapter Twelve

fter speaking with Shannon, I decided to call Bryce. Once again, we talked for hours. Before hanging up, we agreed to meet at the park the next day.

I thought about Bryce all night long and I thought about what Shannon said, and I decided that I was going to keep my age to myself. What he didn't know wouldn't hurt him. I didn't have any expectations, and I knew we were just messing around and I was going to enjoy it.

Stormi 2: You need to keep your business to yourself. If you don't tell people your business you don't have to worry about how they feel about what you're doing. This is your life; live it how you want. It doesn't always pay to be Miss Goody Two

Shoes. When Stormi 1 cracks her mouth about doing the right thing, tell her to go to hell.

I was on my way to the park to meet Bryce. I was having second thoughts; he deserved to know the truth. I got to the park and Bryce was bouncing his basketball on the court. Bryce walked up to me and gave me a big kiss.

The truth just went out the window.

"Hey baby, how are you?"

"I'm doing well, Bryce. How are you doing?"

"Girl, I'm good now that I see you. Let's shoot some hoops."

"Okay."

We shot hoops for about an hour. We took a water break and Bryce asked me if I would like to spend some time with him at his house. I told him that I was all sweaty and needed to change my clothes. He told me not worry that I could wash up at his house. I didn't even take enough time to think about it. I just said, "Okay." We got in his car and headed to his house.

Bryce opened the door for me. "Ladies first!"

The last time I heard that phrase I was walking into a vacant house with James. It brought back so many memories. I walked in and immediately sat on the couch, as I started to feel nervous. Bryce offered me some water after I drank the water and I began to feel relaxed. We sat on the couch watching TV.

"Stormi would you like me to start your shower? While you shower, I will put your clothes in the washer."

"Okay!"

I went into the bathroom and the shower was steaming. Bryce told me to put my dirty clothes on top of the vanity and he would pick them up. I got undressed. I entered the shower and the hot water felt so good. I heard Bryce entering the bathroom and I pulled the shower curtain back. I watched him pick up my clothes and leave a T-shirt for me to wear.

My mind was at peace. I closed my eyes and relaxed as the warm water ran down my body. I just stood there with my eyes closed allowing my mind to drift off.

As I exhaled, I heard the shower curtain open. I felt the cool of the air from outside the shower on my body, but I never opened my eyes. I continued to enjoy the soothing effects of the warm water. Suddenly, I felt the warmth of

Bryce's body next to mine. He was naked. I felt him behind me. I felt his pole of life on my butt. He caressed my breast with the soap, washing my back and my legs. He rubbed me all over. I turned around and pressed my naked body against his, and he kissed me with such passion.

Bryce touched me as if I had never been touched before. He rubbed my jewel box and looked into my eyes, telling me, "I want to take care of *her*." I had no idea what he meant. I just went along with whatever he said. I nodded in agreement.

Bryce got on his knees.

What is he going to do?

He took the soap, rubbed my jewel box, took a shaver, and shaved my jewel box almost bald. He was very gentle. Bryce rinsed me off and told me to dry off and to put the T-shirt on. I got out of the shower, dumbfounded. *What am I going to do with a bald jewel box?*

Bryce washed himself and got out of the shower. I sat on the couch watching TV. Bryce walked over and turned off the TV. He turned on his stereo and played slow jams. I guess that was his way of getting me in the mood. Truth be told, I was already in the mood.

Bryce laid me back on the couch and put a pillow under my butt and he spread my legs far apart.

"It's too soon," I told him.

"Relax, don't worry. I'm going to take good care of her."

I was nervous. I was waiting for him to take off his underwear, but he never did. Bryce put his head between my legs and kissed my jewel box. A slight lick of the tongue going up and down, he kissed the inner parts of my thighs. He licked her and kissed her for at least thirty minutes. I thought I was going to lose my mind. The intensity was amazing. My body began to shake. When Bryce finished, he asked me if I enjoyed it. I was at a loss for words.

Bryce got my clothes out of the dryer and handed them to me. I put on my clothes and he got dressed as well. Bryce made us something to eat; we talked and enjoyed each other's company. Two hours had passed and it was time for Bryce to take me home. On the way home, Bryce held my hand tightly.

"Bryce, why are you holding my hand so tight?"

"Stormi, I'm leaving for school tomorrow. I won't be seeing you after today."

"Is that why you didn't have sex with me?"

"No, I care for you a great deal. You are a beautiful young woman. The timing isn't right for us. You are too young."

"What, how do you know?"

"Stormi, I inquired about you. I know exactly how old you are. I wanted to show you how a real man should treat you. You are more than what's between your legs. I wanted to give you a gift. My gift to you is experience. You know now what to expect from a real man. Keep your jewel box trimmed and sweet, and if he's not willing to eat don't get in the sheets."

Bryce gave me his number at school and told me if I ever needed him, he was just a phone call away. He told me we would be together; our time was in the future. He kissed me on my forehead; the same spot James would kiss me when we first started seeing each other. I was so shocked. He stopped his car at the corner of my street. I got out the car and walked the rest of the way home.

They call me Stormi.

Chapter Thirteen

I didn't know what to do with myself; my experience with Bryce was one no one would ever understand. It was amazing. My mind was all over the place. I couldn't imagine not having him in my life. He would be my friend for life. He made the experience all about me. For once in my life, it was all about making me happy.

I would never sacrifice our friendship by having sex with him, but he could definitely kiss my jewel box again. I didn't even know you could do that. I guess I had a lot to learn.

One more week and I was off to a new school. My mother was sending us to school out of our district. She was going to have to drive to another city for us to go to school. She felt the schools in our neighborhood were changing. Kids were starting to gangbang and she didn't want us exposed to the danger.

I didn't understand because my cousin Nino was a major gangbanger. He was a WDU. He had been shot and now he was in a wheelchair, but he still banged. We were exposed to gang banging within our family. *Well, she had to do what she felt was right.* I couldn't image going to school without my girl Shannon, but I would be going to school with my cousins. We were using their address to go to school out of our area. Going to a new school was going to be a big change, but I was ready for the new experience.

Days had passed and I really wanted to call Bryce, but I thought I should give him some time to settle into school. I was bored and had nothing to do, so I called Joyce to see if she wanted to hang out.

"Hello Joyce, what are you doing?"

"Hey Stormi, I'm watching TV. What's up with you?"

"Girl, I'm bored. Let's walk to the hamburger stand and get some fries."

"Okay Stormi, what time do you want to go?"

"I'm going to put my shoes on and I will be at your house in about ten minutes."

As usual, Joyce was sitting on the porch, waiting for me. We walked to the hamburger stand, ordered fries and shakes. We were sitting outside eating our food when we saw Trent, the guy we met at a party we attended several months ago. He was ordering food.

"Do you remember him?" I asked Joyce.

"Yes, that's that guy Trent that you met at the party."

"You think I should say hello? He gave me his business card, but I never called."

"Stormi he looks like a thug maybe you should leave him be."

"Joyce, you're so scary. I'm going to say hi anyway."

I walked over to Trent and tapped him on his shoulder.

"Hey Trent. How are you doing?"

"Do I know you?"

"Yes, we met at a party a couple of months ago. You gave me your card and told me to call you."

"Yeah, I remember you. How have you been? You never used that card."

"I know, but I still have it. I was going to get around to calling you."

"You do that. I will talk to you a little later."

Trent got his food, got into his '64 Chevy Impala, and drove off. I walked back to where Joyce was sitting.

"Joyce, what do you think he does for a living?"

"I don't know Stormi, but I'm sure it's not legal."

"Girl, he's in the pharmaceutical business."

"Really Stormi? He's a pharmacist?"

"If that's what you want to call it." I laughed.

We finished eating our fries and headed home. I visited with Joyce for about an hour then I headed home. The day was almost over, and it was time for me to check in at home. I went to my room and the first thing I looked for was the card Trent had given me. He was an interesting person. I was going to call him to see what he was all about. I didn't have a physical interest in him; he just appeared to be someone I would want to know. I didn't think it would hurt to have a friend like Trent. One never knew when one might need a Thug! I found the card, but I still didn't feel like talking to him. My mother entered the room.

"Stormi, we have to go shopping for school clothes. I want to take you this weekend."

"Mom, I want to shop for my own clothes. I don't need any help."

"How are you going to get there?"

"I can use your car. I'm just going to the swap meet."

"Let me think about it Stormi, I need to run this past your father. You have two years before you can get your driver's license, and you are driving as if you have it already."

"I know Mom, but I can go to the swap meet and get about six pairs of pants compared to going to the mall and getting three."

" Stormi I know, but will it be the same quality?"

"Mom, I'm going to a new junior high school in Linux. I have to show them how we do it in Corona." I started to laugh so hard. For some reason when people hear you are from Corona, they get scared. I don't know why, Corona is just like any other city. My cousins lived in Corona before they moved to Linux.

"I will let you know Saturday if your father is okay with you driving to the swap meet."

I called my cousin Britney to ask her what the dress code was. She had been living in Linux for a couple of years. She said most people shopped at the mall, and that they didn't have any swap meets in Linux. That gave me an idea of how I planned to dress. I was going to wear what I liked. I refuse to dress like everyone else. The swap meet had polyester pants in every color. I was going to get my black Crocasacks shoes, my Levi's, and my fur boots. *They are not going to be ready for me!*

Stormi 2: Why are you so worried about what people are wearing? You are entering into a new environment. Make sure you have some protection with you. You never know what may happen. This is not your territory. Your father has a box cutter in the garage. Get it and put it in your purse.

I was up early on Saturday morning, hoping my mother was going to let me go shopping. I was in the kitchen, eating cereal with Asia and Valencia. Derrick came in bothering everyone. He pulled Valencia's hair. He kept mess going.

but if you ever had a problem, he was the one you wanted to call. Derrick was ruthless; he was constantly fighting at school. His ass was bad. I didn't know how he was going to survive in a new school. Sending him to a new school might be a mistake.

My mother entered the kitchen and got a cup of coffee. I waited for her to tell me if I could go shopping. She was drinking her coffee and having small talk with Asia and Valencia. I couldn't wait any longer, so I asked her if dad had given permission for me to go shopping alone.

"Stormi, your dad didn't give permission for you to go shopping by yourself. We all are going shopping together. I'm going to use my Montgomery Ward charge card and you will be able to get more things."

"Mom, but the pants I want are at the swap meet."

"I know, Stormi. I saved some money just for your pants. I know how much you wanted all the different colors."

It had been a long day, but we got all the shopping done. My mom was able to get all the pants I wanted. I start school on the following Monday and it was going to be different. I had to meet all new people.

It wouldn't be so bad, as my cousins would be there. My sisters were excited about going to a new school, but Derrick was mad; he didn't want to leave the school he had been attending. That was going to be a problem for my mother. Derrick could be a handful when he didn't want to do something. Hopefully, all would go well. I didn't want to hear my father's mouth. My mother handled most things. She never got my father involved if she didn't have to.

We got up very early Monday morning, and my mother had to drive to Linux. It wasn't that far, but she wanted to time the trip. As I was getting dressed, I had a knot in my stomach. I knew it was just my nerves.

Stormi 1: Today will be a good day. Make sure you say your prayers and keep an open mind. You will meet new people; stay prayed up and positive.

Stormi 2: Don't forget that box cutter; make sure you stay ready and then you won't have to get ready. Keep your eyes open; don't take your guard down. Let people know off the bat that you're not to be messed with. Keep that don't mess with me look on your face; this keeps people confused. They won't be sure how to approach you. You will run into the troublemakers that will try you, but show no fear.

We got to Linux and my mom dropped us off at my aunt's house. She let us know she would be there waiting to pick us up when we got out of school. We walked to school with my cousins. Valencia and Derrick walked with our cousins to elementary school and Asia and I walked with our other cousins to junior high. We got to school early, so I went into the bathroom to put on my eyeliner. My mother wouldn't let me wear makeup, but I wore it anyway. I just had to remember to take it off before she picked me up.

It was a very nice school, not that different from my previous Jr. High. I wore my Levi's and Crocasacks on the first day. The bathroom was filled with girls putting on makeup and lipstick. I took out my Maybelline eye pencil, held it under the hot water, which made it go on darker. My cousin Brittany walked into the bathroom with her friend Teena. Brittany had been attending Linux Junior

High for the last two years, so she was well known.

Brittany was about five-feet-four, one hundred and two pounds, very pretty and could dress her ass off; she always could. She had a good eye for putting clothes together. Her friend Teena was short, fat, and very loud.

Brittany tapped me on the shoulder. "Hey cousin, class is getting ready to start. You ready? We have the same homeroom."

"Yes, I'm ready."

"Cuz, this is my friend Teena."

Teena looked me up and down as though she were sizing me up. I looked at her and gave her a nod.

"So, Brittany tells me you're from Corona."

"If that's what Brittany told you then I guess it must be true."

"That's what she told me, but I'm asking you."

"Don't ask me something that my cousin already gave the answer to. You don't need to know where I'm from. It's not your concern!"

"You don't have to be so mean! I just wanted to ask you what's it like living in Corona."

"Really? Well check this out. I'm not from another planet. You have known my cousin for two years. If you wanted to know about Corona then you should have asked her."

"Why would she know about Corona?"

"Because she grew up there!"

"Oh, she never told me that."

"Whatever!"

Brittany and I walked to our homeroom, went inside, and took a seat. Everyone was walking up to Brittany, asking her what she did for the summer. She introduced me to her friends.

It was time for lunch, and I made it through my first classes. I looked for Asia; I wanted to make sure she was okay. I was walking around and saw my other cousin Shelia. We all joined up and looked for Asia. I was sure Asia was okay. She was most likely with our cousin Destiny, as they were the same age.

I sat on top of the lunch table, waiting to see Asia. Asia saw me and walked up.

"Hey little sis, how is it going?"

"It's okay. Everyone is really nice. Destiny has introduced me to a lot of people."

I sat back and checked everyone out, trying not to say too much. I just listened to what people were saying. I found if you stopped and just listened to people, you would soon see what they were all about. I already knew I didn't like Teena's fat butt!

I made it through the first day. Before leaving school, I went into the bathroom to take the eyeliner off my eyes.

I met up with everyone and we walked to the house. As soon as we hit the block, I saw my mother's car. She had already picked up Valencia and Derrick from school.

"Hey Stormi, how was your first day at school?"

"It was okay!"

"Just okay?"

"Yes, Mom, nothing special; it's just school."

"Asia how was your first day?"

"I met a lot of new people; I had a good day. Everyone was so friendly and I like all of my teachers."

My mother knew I didn't want to change schools, so I really didn't have that much to say.

When I got home, I did my homework and my chores done. The phone rang and it was Brittany.

"Hey Stormi, I need to talk to you about Teena."

"What about her?"

"She thinks you were rude to her."

"What? I don't care what her fat butt thinks."

"Well Stormi, she comes from a very large family of sisters and they run the school."

"So what, are you scared of them, is that why you hang with her fat butt?"

"It's just easier to be with them than not."

"Well you can forget it. I'm not kissing nobody's butt. I don't care how many sisters she has. She better not step to me."

"Stormi, it is not wise messing with them, trust me. You're not a fighter."

"No, I'm not, but I will if I have to."

"Trust me; you don't want to take on this family. Just be nice to her and you will be fine. I will see you tomorrow."

That was some crazy shit. Now I had to worry about some ugly fat girl. I couldn't believe it.

Stormi 2: I know you're not that big on fighting, but you did do a good job fighting Reese. I suggest you continue to take that box cutter to school. The time is going to come when you may have to defend yourself.

I couldn't believe I had to worry about something else. I wanted to call Shannon, but it was not my day.

Stormi 2: Whatever you do, show no fear.

It was day two at Linux Junior High. I went to the bathroom to put on my eyeliner. I sat my book bag on the counter. I was pulling my bottom eyelid down to draw the line on, and I saw Teena's face in the mirror. I got uneasy. She stood behind me with three other girls. I assumed they were her sisters. I could feel it in my spirit that they were going to do something to me. I couldn't fight all three.

"What's up, Stormi?"

I turned and looked at Teena, but I didn't say a word I grabbed my book bag; the box cutter was in the side zipper. I hoped I could get to it in time. The other three girls surrounded me.

"What kind of name is Stormi?" Teena asked.

"You would have to ask my father."

"I don't have to ask yo' daddy, you tell me. Why do you come in here every morning and put your makeup on?"

I didn't respond to any of her questions. I kept my eyes on all four of them. I didn't want to pull the box cutter out. They might have taken it from me. I didn't know what to do or say.

"You know Stormi; I don't like your ass. I hope your cousin told you what happens to people I don't like."

"I don't care that you don't like me. That's your problem not mine."

Teena reached back and slapped me. I was in shock. I just stood there and let that fat bitch hit me. I didn't do anything. The other three pushed me around and Teena laughed and walked away.

I felt the tears running down my face; the eyeliner started to run. I looked at myself in the mirror and I was disgusted with myself. I should have fought back. She was going to mess with me every time she saw me.

The bell rang for homeroom. I washed my face and re-applied my eyeliner. My cheek was red from the slap.

I grabbed my book bag and went to class. I sat at my desk and tried to act as if nothing happened. I met up with my cousins for lunch and I never mentioned what happened.

They call me Stormi.

Chapter Fourteen

Several months passed and I was still dealing with the same mess from Teena and her sisters. I didn't tell anyone. I didn't want them to know that I let her get away with slapping me. They tormented me whenever they could. I even stopped going to the bathroom in the morning.

Stormi 2: This has to stop! I don't care how scared you are, you have to fight back. You can't let people push you around. You have to catch them one by one. They feel strong when they are together, but they are weak by themselves. You take the box cutter and threaten to cut their throats they will leave you alone, trust me. This is the only way you will stop them from bullying you.

Stormi 1: You should tell an adult what's going on. You can tell your mother and she will handle this for you. There is no need for you to walk around in fear. You can also tell a school official.

Hiding from Teena made the hours at school go by slow. I was tired of hiding. I decided to watch her and her crew while they were not watching me. I made a list of each of their classes. I created a timeline, charting the times they were not together. I tricked my cousin Brittany into giving me Teena's telephone number. I monitored them for three weeks. When I made my move, they would regret they had ever met me.

The day had come, and it was time for me to make my move. I decided to get them all on the same day. I learned that Teena had a weak bladder; she got a pass to go to the bathroom at two o'clock every day. I planned to be there waiting on her.

I was watching the clock. It was 1:55 p.m., and I asked the teacher for a bathroom pass. I hid in the bathroom, waiting on Teena. I entered the first stall and I stood on the toilet, so she wouldn't be able to see my feet. I heard her fat thighs rubbing together, as she entered the bathroom.

Teena opened the stall; I jumped off the toilet, and grabbed her fat ass by the throat. She was in shock. I took my box cutter and held to her neck.

"Bitch, you are going to wish you never met me," I said, pushing her into the wall, pressing the box cutter against her neck. "Don't say a word to me or I will cut your neck. You should have never slapped me." I punched her in the stomach and, of course, she pissed on herself. She begged me to stop, but I had no mercy on her.

I slapped her in the face. "If you ever touch me again I will kill you."

She saw the fire in my eyes and she begged and pleaded with me, as tears ran down her face, but I had no mercy on her. My rage was unbelievable. I grabbed her hair and cut a piece off with the box cutter. I placed it in a plastic bag.

"I will put a curse on you if you even look at me funny."

She was begging me to stop, but I couldn't. I grabbed her arm, pulled up her sleeve, and carved an X in her arm. The cut wasn't deep, but just deep enough to make her bleed. She apologized to me. Teena was sobbing like a big baby. I let her know that I planned to get her little sisters, too. She begged me not to hurt them. "They only did it because I made them do it," she said. She guaranteed me that I didn't have to worry about them. I decided to give her sisters a pass.

Teena was no longer a problem. She was hanging out with me now. I had made some new friends and things were going good at school. I had my eye on this guy name Jermaine. He was tall and thin, and a cutie. He was very articulate and funny. I had him in a couple of my classes. We joked and played around with each other. I had seen him at some of the ditch parties. We definitely liked each other, but we had not officially made it known. The school hosted a Sports Night once a month for all ninth graders. We were half way through the school year and I had not attended any, but I planned to be at the next one.

The week was going by fast, soon Friday would be here and it would be time for Sports Night. I had no idea what I was going to wear. I was at home going through my closet, trying to put something together when in walked my mother.

"What are you doing, Stormi?"

"The school is a having a Sports Night on Friday and I would like to attend, but I can't figure out what to wear."

"Well, let me help you. Pull out your black suit and put your red blouse underneath. I think this will look nice. I have the perfect shoes for this outfit."

My mom went to her closet and returned with some beautiful red suede shoes with a black bow and a red hat to match with a black feather on the side. She put the ensemble together on the bed.

"Mom, I can really wear this on Friday?"

"Of course you can. I have been waiting on this day. I can't wait to dress you up. You will definitely be a showstopper."

"Thank you Mom."

I couldn't wait to call Shannon to tell her about the dance. I wished she were here to share in my joy. It was almost time for her to deliver the baby; she had one more month to go. I had saved some money to buy my godchild a gift. Once the baby was born, Shannon was moving back. I couldn't wait to see her and the baby. I hoped it was a girl.

It was Friday and all of the ninth graders were excited about Sports Night. My mother was going to drop all the cousins off and pick us up after the dance. Once I got dressed, I looked nice. My mother's shoes and hat made the outfit.

We went to pick up my cousins. They all walked out and looked simply beautiful. They got into the car and we headed for the dance. My mother dropped us off in front of the school.

We all walked into the dance; everyone looked very nice. I didn't see Jermaine. I guessed he hadn't made it yet. Teena walked up to me with the rest of the girls and we hung out around the punch table. I felt a tap on my shoulder. It was Jermaine.

"Hello Stormi, would you like to dance?"

"Yes!"

They were playing one of my favorite songs by Parliament Funkadelic! Jermaine and I were dancing and having a good time. After dancing three records, Jermaine walked me outside to get some air. We sat on the bench.

"Stormi, you look nice tonight. I like your hat. It looks good on you."

"Thanks Jermaine."

"Stormi are you seeing anyone?"

"No, I'm not."

"Will you consider being my girlfriend?"

"Yes, I will be your girlfriend."

Jermaine leaned in to kiss me. It was nice. We went back into the dance and had a great time. I didn't want Jermaine to know I was excited, so I played it cool. Jermaine was a great guy. This would be the first time I had dated someone my own age. I was going to let my mom know what was going on this time. *No more sneaking around.*

The dance was over and I gave Jermaine a kiss on the cheek. I gathered my cousins and we went to the meeting spot. Of course, my mother was sitting waiting on us.

We got in the car and headed home. I had a great time at the dance. I planned to talk to my mom about Jermaine when I got up tomorrow. I got undressed and put on my pajamas. I lay in my bed thinking about Jermaine and I decided to call Bryce.

"Hello, may I speak to Bryce?"

"Just a minute."

"Hello, Bryce speaking."

"Hey baby! Whatcha doing?"

"Stormi, is that you?"

"Yes, I thought I would let you get settled before I called you."

"Girl, it has been months, well over six. What's happening with you?"

"Nothing much; you were on my mind and I thought I would give you a call. By the way, I have my own phone now. Well, actually, I have to share with my siblings, but you can call me now. Things have changed around here. I have a lot more freedom. I'm going to school in Linux."

"How do you like your new school?"

"It's okay. At first, I was a having a hard time, but things worked themselves out. What's going on with you? Do you have a girlfriend?"

"No, I'm too busy for that; besides, I left my girlfriend at home, Stormi!"

"I wish I were your girlfriend. I want to talk to you about someone."

"Who?"

"There's this guy at school; he asked me to be his girlfriend."

"What did you tell him, Stormi?"

"I said yes, but I want to know what you think."

"I think you have some growing to do. I feel that your education should be your priority. You have already experienced two older guys, your friend James that took advantag of you, and me. I, on the other hand, thought you and I were the same age. I did my research and found that you were not age appropriate. I should have walked away, but it was something about you. Even though we didn't have sex, we engaged in a sexual act and I was wrong for that. In actuality, I was no better than James was. You are now dealing with someone your own age; most boys your age are immature and lack experience. Stormi, don't move too fast, and remember what I taught you. A real man will respect your body. Be careful, baby girl! Let me know how it goes. I will talk to you soon."

Bryce was so amazing. I felt bad that I tried to deceive him. I guess I was only thinking of myself. I felt like I wanted to move forward with Jermaine, but this time I would do it the right way. No more sneaking around, I would be truthful with my mother. I believed she would understand. As I lay in my bed, I dozed off and the phone rang. It was Jermaine.

"Hello Stormi, how are you?"

"I'm doing very well, Jermaine. Why are you up at this time of night?"

"Well you told me you are a night owl, so I took a chance on calling you. I thought you would still be up."

"Yes, I'm still up, but I did doze off."

"I just wanted to let you know I had a great time with you tonight. I really liked your outfit."

"Thanks so much Jermaine, I enjoyed you as well. You drew a lot of attention when you walked in the door with that Maxie coat on; you looked nice also.

"Stormi, what are you doing tomorrow?"

"I don't have anything planned. I was going to sit down and have a conversation with my mom in regards to us. I want to make sure I get her permission to date. I want everything to be on the up and up."

"How do you think she is going to respond?"

"I don't know; we had already discussed dating and she told me I could date at fifteen, but I'm going to try and convince her to push the age back to fourteen. I'm very mature; I haven't given her any problems. I'm going to plead my case. I don't want to have to sneak around. I'm not up for the drama!"

"Well, I was going to invite you to a pool party at Joey's house."

"That sounds like fun. I will call you after I speak with my mom and if everything goes well, I may meet you there."

"Alright Stormi, you have a good night. I will talk to you tomorrow."

"Bye, Jermaine."

They call me Stormi.

Chapter Fifteen

❦

*E*verything was going great with Jermaine. I was grateful that my mother trusted me enough to allow me to date. I was doing well in school and had no problems at home. Shannon had a baby girl and would be returning home in the summer. Time was flying. I would soon be graduating from junior high school and on my way to high school.

My relationship with Jermaine was getting intense; he wanted more, thinking we should go to the next level. I was not sure if that's what I wanted. I was perfectly okay with a little bump and grind, and finger banging. He had asked me several times to come over to his house during school hours. A friend of ours was having a ditch party on Friday, and I knew Jermaine was going to press the issue.

Stormi 1: You have been down this road before. Don't allow anyone to pressure you into doing something you shouldn't be doing. Don't forget what you learned in your purity class keep yourself for your husband. God is your source; go back and read your Bible. The word of God will give you what you need. Don't give in.

The week was ending and I had to decide what I was going to do. I liked Jermaine and I knew if I didn't give it up, he wouldn't mess with me anymore. I had to meet Jermaine after his basketball practice was over, and I would have had it figured out by then. The lunch bell had just rang, and I was going to meet my cousins for lunch.

Brittany and Sheila were waiting on me. I got to the table and the first thing that came out of their mouths was, "Are you going to the ditch party?"

"I don't know. I'm thinking about it. Are you going, Brittany?"

"I'm going if you go. JoJo asked me to come, but I told him I have to think about it. I know if I go, we are taking it to the next level for sure, and I need to prepare myself for that. Shelia, are you coming?"

"Yes, I'm going. Larry and I have already taken it to the next level. We have been dating much longer than you all have. It's no big deal for us. I'm going to have a good time."

I'm not shocked about Shelia and Larry; they had been going strong for almost two years. She met him when they first moved to Linux and they had been a couple ever since. Well, I guess I needed to make up my mind because Jermaine was waiting for an answer today.

Stormi 2: Don't forget what Bryce taught you. If a guy isn't willing to eat, don't get into the sheets!

I met Jermaine after his basketball practice. I let him know I would be at the ditch party. He had a big smile on his face. I, on the other hand, didn't feel I was ready, but I was going to do it anyway. Bryce's voice was ringing in my head. *If he don't eat no sheets.* Jermaine would have to pass the test.

It was Friday and everyone that was invited to the ditch party was there, including my cousins. We were sitting around talking and laughing and all the couples had put their names in a hat. The host pulled the names of the first four couples. They were given their room assignment. The house had five bedrooms, but the parents' room was off limits.

I was hoping we were in the first four, this way I knew we would be on clean sheets. Brittany and JoJo names were called first. The second couple was called and then the third. Finally, the names of the fourth couple—"Jermaine and Stormi."

I was glad our name was pulled for the first round. We got our room assignment and the rules that went along with the room. *This must have been going on for a long time because it was so organized.* Jermaine and I headed to our room.

Stormi 2: Don't forget!

I was a little nervous, not because I was scared to do it, but because I didn't want to have to ask him to eat my sweet meat! He should have already known what to do. We sat on the bed, and start kissing, and touching each other. He took off his clothes and then I took off my top and then my pants. I had on my bra and panties. He rubbed between my thighs. My jewel box was getting wet. I was feeling sexy. I rubbed his pole of life and it was a decent size. He kissed my neck, and sucked on my breasts. I was feeling him, and this was going good. I straddled him and started grinding on his pole of life. He was getting excited. I took off my bra and panties. He knew I was ready, as he got on top of me. He kissed my neck and then he moved down to my breasts. This was going good. He kissed my stomach and then I felt him getting ready to put his pole of life inside of me. I put my arms around his head and pushed his head down toward my jewel box.

"Kiss her Jermaine. Lick her until she screams!"

"Stormi, what are you doing? Where did you learn that?"

"What do you mean where did I learn that, you don't kiss?"

"No, I don't put my face in pussy! Are you a virgin?"

"Why Jermaine does it matter?"

"Yes it does. I only date virgins."

"Well, it doesn't matter if I'm a virgin or not. If you don't eat, no sheets."

Jermaine jumped up and got dressed.

"I'm not fucking you Stormi; it's obvious someone already did."

"You don't know what someone has done, and it's obvious you don't know what you're doing."

Jermaine left the room, and I got dressed. It was hard to believe what just happened, but whatever, life goes on. I guess my experience with Bryce was valuable; it taught me how to separate the boys from the men.

It was early Monday morning and I always hooked up with Jermaine for breakfast before we went to class. I was not sure how today was going to go. I hadn't heard from him all weekend and he refused to take my calls. He was so immature. I was sitting on the bench, eating my breakfast and Brittany and Shelia came over.

"Hey, Stormi."

"Hey Brit, hey Shelia, have you guys seen Jermaine?"

Brittany had a strange look on her face and Shelia pointed at a table in the back of the cafeteria. I looked behind me and Jermaine was hugged up with someone else. What was he doing? I didn't know the girl he was hugged up with, but I had seen her around. Everyone at this school knew we were together; she was wrong for that. I tried to act as if it didn't bother me, but it did.

I held my head up and went to class. The bell rang and it was time for our lunch break. I met up with Brittany, Shelia, Teena and some other friends. We were sitting on the grass, talking. The first thing that came up was what happened at the ditch party. I was listening to what was being said and it was obvious that Jermaine told everyone what happened and because no one was familiar with kissing the jewel box, it was a big deal.

I told my friends, "Fuck what they think."

As we walked off the yard, we passed a group of girls and one of them happened to be the girl that was hugged up with Jermaine that morning.

"Hey, Stormi, I hear you're a porn star. You like to have your pussy licked."

"What did you say, bitch? Did you call me a porn star? Fuck you."

"No, Stormi, fuck you. You are a freak; no one licks pussy."

"Bitch, no one licks your pussy. Keep talking and I will fuck you up."

"Stormi, you just mad because I have your man. No one is into that freaky shit; you must be a hoe."

"No, bitch, yo' mama is a hoe and I will show your ass how big of a hoe she is after school."

I was considered a hoe because they're scared to eat the jewel box; this is crazy. Jermaine was wrong for putting my business in the streets and he was going to pay for it. *Damn, now I had to fight that bitch after school.*

By fourth period, it was all over the school that I was going to be fighting. The sad part about it was that I didn't even know the girl's name. I met up with my cousins on our break and Brittany told me the girl's name was Charmaine and she came from a big family. She had older sisters that attended Worthington High school.

I had no choice but to fight. On our next break, I had Brittany braid my hair down so I could tie my bandana around my head. I was feeling a little anxious.

Stormi 1: The Word of God says, "In all things pray." You have nothing to prove; never mind what people are saying about you. God is a God of love. Walk away from this fight. Allow God to fight your battles.

Deep down inside I didn't want to fight, but I have learned that sometimes you have to. I had to fight Reese and I had to fight Teena. People tend to push me around, well, not anymore. I would use the same strategy I used with Reese, I will tell her, I don't want to fight and when her guard was down, I was going to take her down.

That may have seemed underhanded, but it was a fight—nothing is fair in war.

I got ready to go to my last class and the hallways were filled with people gossiping about the fight. As I walked through, people were patting me on my back. I had sense enough to know that they didn't care about me; they just wanted to see a fight. I was sure they were patting Charmaine on her back as well.

Jermaine was coming my way. He walked by me, as if he hadn't noticed me. I was pissed off. I was fighting because he was an inexperienced boy afraid of what he knew nothing about.

Stormi 2: This fight has to take place. Jermaine wants to run his mouth and talk about you. Well you make sure you show him who's boss. You beat her ass and let him know you're coming for him next. You have to get the upper hand; rush her as if you're a bull and don't stop until she's on the ground.

When the bell rang, I met up with my sister and cousins in front of the school. There were crowds of people standing around. I headed to the end of the block, away from the school. Charmaine was already at the corner, standing with her friends.

My heart was beating so fast. All I could think of was I needed to beat her ass. The closer I got to her, the more anxious I got. All of a sudden, I got a burst of energy and I took off running and ran dead into her. I hit her so hard she hit the ground, with no time to recover. I jumped on top of her and continued to hit her in her face. The crowd was out of control, as they pushed to get closer. Charmaine was trying to get up, but I wouldn't let her. I heard her friend yelling for me to get off her. I continued to hit her in her face. She began to bleed profusely. I got scared, so I stopped hitting her. Brittany helped me up; Charmaine was being helped up also. The next thing I knew Asia ran up and hit her in the face. She fell and hit the pavement. I grabbed Asia's hand, and we ran as fast as we could. Brittany, Teena, Shelia, and Destiny were all running alongside of us.

We never looked back. We ran all the way to my cousin's house. As soon as we arrived, I saw my mother waiting for us.

"What's going on? Why are you running and why are you soaked in blood?"

"Mom, I was supposed to have a fight with this girl at school but the crowd started pushing and she got trampled."

"Oh my God! Stormi, get into the car."

My mother drove me back to the school and we saw that Charmaine was being put into the ambulance. I was scared. My mother parked the car and told me to get out. I refused.

"Stormi, you get out of this car! We are going into this school to deal with this."

The police were everywhere. I was petrified. I got out of the car slowly. My mother came around to my side of the car, grabbed my hand, and pulled me out the car. We walked into the school office. My mother told the office assistant that we needed to speak with the principal. When we got to the principal's office, my mother told the principal that I was one of the girls that had been fighting. The principal asked me what happened.

Stormi 2: You have the upper hand. Don't admit to anything and lie about everything.

"Young lady, can you tell me what happened?"

"I don't know what happened. Charmaine and I were talking and the next thing I knew I was being hit upside my head, the crowd was pushing, and Charmaine fell on the ground. I believe the crowd trampled her. It became a free-for-all and everyone started hitting each other. I started running and ran all the way home."

"Well, we are going to have to get to the bottom of this. Until I find out what took place, you are on suspension for the rest of the week."

I gathered my things from my locker and my mother took me home.

Stormi 2: Stick to your story!

My mother was extremely upset; she barely said one word.

When we arrived home, my mother told me to go take a bath. As I was running the bath water, Asia walked in.

"Stormi, are you going to tell Mommy that I hit that girl?"

"Asia, don't worry about it; you had my back. I told Mommy that Charmaine and I were talking and someone hit me in the head, the crowd got out of control and Charmaine ended up on the ground and that the crowd trampled her. You just stick to that story."

"Okay Stormi."

I got into the tub and my body felt like it had been through a war; my muscles were very sore. My mother knocked on the door and came in while I was soaking.

"What's the name of the young lady you fought? I want to call the hospital and check on her.

"Mom her name is Charmaine, but we didn't have a fight. I was hit in the head and she was trampled."

"Whatever, I just need to check and make sure she is okay. You can be charged with assault. I just called your aunt. She called her lawyer friend, and he said it depends on what happens after the investigation. If they find you at fault they can charge you."

Stormi 2: Stick with the story; don't get scared.

I was suddenly sick to my stomach. I got out of the tub and got into my bed. Asia was sitting on her bed. She was worried sick. She was rocking back and forth.

"Asia, stop rocking. You are stressing me out. It's going to be okay."

Valencia walked into the room.

"Why don't you get on your knees and pray God hears your prayers."

Asia jumped out of her bed, got on her knees and prayed. I listened to her pray. I actually prayed in my head. I had to stick to the story. I couldn't act as if I had done anything wrong.

My mother walked in the room to let me know that Charmaine had been released from the hospital and that she was okay. That's a heavy load off my mind. I never really wanted to fight, but I had no choice. I hoped after the investigation, I could return to school.

The investigation was over and I could return to school. No one gave the police any information, so there was nothing they could do. Charmaine's sisters sent word to me that they were going to get me.

When I returned to school, I had a large fan club — people I didn't even know wanted to hang with me because they thought that I could fight. Every day someone walked up to me, offering to buy my lunch. I became very popular and Asia was known for her knockout punch.

Jermaine was now seeing Charmaine. That hurt me. After all, I went through, she still ended up with him. I would see Charmaine around campus and she would stare at me and point her finger. I knew it wasn't over; we would have to fight again.

Several weeks had passed and things were starting to get back to normal. It would soon be time for graduation.

Thank God, it was Friday! It was early in the morning and I was on my way to homeroom. Before I could enter class, Brittany grabbed my arm and pulled me to the side.

"Stormi, don't go to your homeroom this morning."

"Why, what's wrong?"

"I heard some girls in the bathroom talking. They didn't know I was in the stall. Charmaine's sisters are coming to jump on us today."

"What?"

"Yes, I heard them say they will be waiting for us after school. What are we going to do?"

"Calm down, Brittany, it's going to be okay. Let's go."

"Where are we going?"

"We're going to ride the bus to Corona and go get our cousin Nino. They are not going to ambush us."

Brittany and I rode the bus to Corona. We found Nino and told him what was going on. Nino was in a wheelchair after being shot in his back, but that didn't stop him from gang banging. Nino's homeboy put him in the car and told us to get in. They drove us back to school. We waited at the park until school was out.

The last bell rang. We got into the car and drove to the front of the school. Nino was sitting in the back of the car. I noticed a bunch of girls hanging on the corner. Nino told Brittany and me to get out the car. He opened the back door and placed his gun on the seat. Nino's homeboy got of out the car with his gun in his belt. The gun was visible.

Nino told his homeboy to walk us down to where the girls were. I felt a sense of security, as I walked with my head up. Brittany was even walking strong. Nino's homeboy was about six-foot-five and very scary looking. As usual, everyone was gathered around waiting for the fight. I saw Charmaine and her sisters, but all they saw was the gun.

"Who came to fight Stormi and Brittany?"he asked.

No one said a word.

"I'm here to let you know if you have a problem with them, you have a problem with me."

You could see the fear in everyone's face. *I'm sure half of them had never even seen a gun.* The crowd started to disburse.

Jermaine walked up to me. "Can I call you later?" he asked.

They call me Stormi.

Chapter Sixteen

I graduated from junior high, and made it through the summer without drama. Because of the fight last year, my mother was now sending me back to school in my own neighborhood. I will be attending Corona High School. I was looking forward to going. I will be with all my friends. I was extremely happy because Shannon had returned home and I had my best friend back.

It was the first day of school; I was getting ready to walk out the front door when my mother stopped me. She asked me to sit down. I was puzzled. I knew it was my first day of high school and we had already had the talk about being responsible, nevertheless I sat down.

My mother told me that my father had been messing around with a lady named Babette and that she was sitting outside. She told me to walk to school and to ignore her if she said anything to me.

I got mad; I wanted to kick my father's ass. *What was he thinking, messing around on my mother? She didn't deserve that.* My mother was talking to me but I didn't hear a thing she said. I pictured myself slapping the shit out of my father, but since I couldn't slap my father, I would have to fuck up this lady named Babette. To please my mother, I agreed not to say anything to her, but I couldn't wait to get outside.

I opened the door and I didn't see anyone. I crossed the street and went to Shannon's house so we could walk to school together. I knocked on the door and her mother let me in. Shannon's baby girl was sitting in the high chair and Shannon was feeding her. She was such a beautiful baby; it was hard to believe King's ugly ass was her father. Shannon got her book bag and we walked to school. We stopped to get Joyce.

As we walked to school, I noticed a black car driving slowly behind us. I told Shannon and Joyce what was going on just in case it was Babette. I told them what my mother told me about the situation and they had a look of shock on their faces. I told them to keep walking and not to pay any attention to the car. The car sped off.

We entered the gates of Corona High; people were everywhere. I finally felt like a teenager.

My first day of high school was great. I met new people and spent time with old friends. The school was huge; it was going to take some time for me to find my way around. My mother and my aunt graduated from Corona High so I was keeping the tradition in the family.

It was the end of the school day. Shannon, Joyce, and I were walking home. We got to our block and saw a police car at my house. My heart started racing. I ran to my house and Shannon and Joyce were running alongside of me. My mother and father were standing outside talking to the police. My mother walked over to us and told me everything was okay, and sent my friends home.

I walked in the house. I knew the police being there had something to do with that lady named Babette. I was anxious. I hoped my mother was going to explain to me what happened; she couldn't just tell me that everything was okay and expect me to believe it. I went to my room, Asia and Valencia were sitting on the bed, crying.

"What's wrong with y'all?"

Valencia ran up to me and wrapped her arms around me, holding me tight. She didn't say a word. Valencia rarely spoke; she was a quiet child. She was well behaved and never talked back. She was very calm and sweet. I had never seen her frightened like this before. I held her tight and asked her again what happened, but she refused to speak.

"Asia, what happened? Tell me what happened."

Asia sat on the bed and just sobbed. She had nothing to say. Asia always had something to say. I had to find out what had my family so traumatized! I sat Valencia on the bed and I went looking for Derrick, he would tell me what happened. I found Derrick in his room, sitting on his bed.

"Derrick, what happened?"

"Mom picked us up from school. When we got home, Dad was standing outside talking to this woman. Mom parked the car and we got out, she told us to go into the house. Before we could make it into the house, Mom walked over to Dad and they started arguing. The woman got in Mom's face and the next thing I knew Mom hit her in the mouth. Dad tried to pull them apart, but Mom wouldn't let go. Dad was yelling for us to go into the house, but we didn't, we ran over to help Mom. Mom had the woman on the ground, beating her ass and Dad pulled her off. Asia and Valencia started kicking her and Dad was yelling for me to help him. I pulled Asia and Valencia off of her and she got up off the ground. She started yelling at Dad 'Tell your family you're with me!' I saw the hurt in mom's eyes and before I knew it, I had socked the lady in her face. She hit the ground and didn't wake up. Mom rushed us into the house and the next thing I knew the ambulance was loading her up and taking her away. Do you think I'm going to jail, Stormi?"

"No, Derrick, you're not going to jail. Everything is going to be alright. Don't worry about it. I'm going to go check on Mom; you go and sit with Asia and Valencia."

I stood in the window watching my mother and father talking to the police. My father allowed a stranger to come to our home and insult my mother. *I was so mad at him; I believe that if he said the wrong thing to me, I would explode on him.*

Stormi 1: People make mistakes you have to learn how to forgive, don't judge what you don't know. God is a God of forgiveness, your father obviously made a mistake but he is still your father. He has to deal with his sin it is not for you to judge. In all things, remain prayerful.

Stormi 2: Girl you know what you have to do, you need to lay hands on that bitch. You can't allow someone to come and disrespect your mother. People will fuck with you as long as you let them. You have learned that lesson from Reese, Teena, and Charmaine; there comes a time when you just got to beat a bitch's ass.

My mother came in the house while my father remained outside talking to the police.

"Mom are you okay?"

"I'm okay Stormi. Everything is going to be okay, don't worry about me. Where are your sisters and your brother?"

"They're in the room."

My mother headed to the bedroom where my sisters and brother were. I followed behind her. She entered the room and they ran to hug her. I stood in the doorway, thinking about how that woman had hurt my family. I vowed that I would get Babette.

My mother reassured us that everything was going to be okay but I didn't believe it. She told us not to worry. I had dealt with crazy people before and I was sure as my name was Stormi that Babette would be back and when she came back, I would have something for her ass.

Everyone settled down and my mother prepared dinner. We moved forward as if nothing happened. I just didn't understand how we could all just walk around as if everything was normal. After dinner, I did my homework, took a bath, and went to bed. I was emotionally drained.

I woke up early, I went into the kitchen for a glass of water, and my mother was standing in the living room window.

"Good morning, Mom."

"Good morning, Stormi. Why are you up so early?"

"I guess because I went to bed early. Why are you standing in the window?"

"Well, Babette was released from the hospital last night and she has been circling the house for hours."

"What? Are you serious? She must be crazy. Where is dad?"

"He went to file a police report."

"Mom, why don't you just call Aunt Bebe, she will handle this for you."

"Stormi, this is a family matter. You can't involve your aunt in your dad's and I personal business."

"Aunt Bebe was mom's sister. She use to raise hell back in the day, but she got saved. She still didn't take any shit though. If she knew what was going on she would be here in a heartbeat, and Babette's ass would be missing.

My mother knew that if she called her sister all hell was going to break loose. I didn't understand why she was trying to keep it to herself. Aunt Bebe was family and she would have handled that shit. Back in the day, they called her Pistol Packing "B" she didn't take any shit. She calmed down when she found the Lord.

Stormi 2: If you can't call your aunt then you must handle this yourself. Call your cousin Nino and have him give you a gun. You are going to have to stand up for your family; it's up to you.

Stormi 1: Your father is doing the right thing by going to the police. Let the grown folks handle this; you will find yourself in a world of trouble if you try to handle this. This is God's fight. Stand down!

I was going to honor my mother's wishes and not contact Aunt Bebe, but I was not going to promise that I would stand down. I was going to call my cousin. I wasn't going to ask for a gun, but I was going to talk to him about the situation.

When I was ready to walk out of the door, my mother told me that Babette was still circling the house, but she pled with me to ignore her.

"Stormi, if you see her don't say anything, just continue walking to school. Your father is getting a restraining order."

"What's that?"

"A restraining order is an order of protection from the court. It is a court order restricting her not to be able to come within one hundred feet of the house."

"Okay Mom, if you say so, I will just ignore her if I see her."

"Thanks Stormi. This will be resolved by the time you get home from school."

I walked out of the door and Shannon was waiting on me. We proceeded to walk to school. Joyce was waiting for us at the corner. I told my girls what was going on. Before we could get off the block, that same car from yesterday was following us.

The woman in the car slowed down and rolled down her window. Shannon told me to keep walking and Joyce grabbed my arm. I tried to ignore her.

"How you doing Stormi?"

That bitch knew my name! We continued walking to school.

That crazy bitch called my name again.

"Stormi! You look just like your father. He's always talking about you and your sisters. I'm so glad we finally get to meet. I just wanted to let you know when your dad moves out, it's okay for you and your sisters to come visit him."

"That's it, you crazy backyard bitch, I don't know who let you off your leash but I'm going to fuck you up. Do you really think I'm going to let you get away with fucking with my family?"

I ran over to her car and kicked her car door. I tried to pull her ass out of the car, but Shannon and Joyce grabbed me and pulled me away, and she sped off.

Joyce informed me that she had gotten her license plate number and that I could file harassment. I got the number from her and we continued to walk to school. I did not intend to file charges; I was going to give her license plate number to my cousin. He had a friend that worked at the DMV. *I needed her home address.*

All day long, I thought about Babette. I couldn't concentrate on my class work. *How could my father do this to my mother? How could he do this to our family?*

She knew my name. The more I thought about it the angrier I became. My father was going to leave us for that animal. My emotions were all over the place and I felt out of control. I was fucking mad!

I got up from my desk and walked out of the class. I went outside and walked around. I was walking in circles. I had no control of what I was doing. What was wrong with me? *God, help me; I'm tripping. I can't get a hold of myself.* My heart was racing and I was sweating. I took a deep breath and tried to calm down. I sat down on a bench and began to breathe in and out. I was scared! I didn't know what to do. I ditched the rest of my classes. *No more school for me today, I can't handle it.*

While I was sitting on the bench, two guys sat down beside me, one of them pulled out a joint and started smoking. My head was hung low on the table.

"How you doing lady?"

I looked up and saw this nice looking brother looking at me.

"What's your name?"

"Stormi"

"Girl, I'm scared of that name. My name is Cameron and this is my homeboy Tyrone. "Why you not in class?"

I answered sarcastically. "The same reason you not in class."

They laughed.

"You want to hit this joint?"

"Why not, I don't have anything to lose?"

I needed something to take my mind off of today. I had always passed up the opportunity to get high, but today I made an exception to my rule. I needed to forget what happened this morning. I was not handling my emotions well and nothing made sense. I couldn't believe my father was going to leave us.

Cameron passed me the joint and I took a long, hard drag. I started choking and coughing.

"Girl, you going to be so high, this shit right here will have you just right."

He was right. I was high as hell, but I felt damn good. I didn't know this was how weed made you feel. I was always against smoking, especially after what happened to Shannon. I knew this was wrong, but it felt alright. It made me feel better about my situation.

The bell rang and school was out. I had to meet Shannon and Joyce after school so we could walk home. Cameron let me know that he would be there every day at third period if I wanted to smoke with him. I just gave him a nod. As I walked out of the gate with my girls to go home, James pulled up in his car. I hadn't seen him in a while; he looked good. I watched him as he got out the car and opened the passenger door for some random ass chick. He leaned over and kissed her. I started laughing and thinking to myself, another *one bites the dust*. James was still chasing that young jewel box.

I got home from school and I was extremely hungry. I forgot that you get the munchies from smoking weed. It did ease my stress, though. I guess it was not so bad. I didn't tell my mother what happened with Babette. I felt she had had enough to deal with. I still couldn't believe my father was going to leave his family. What were we going to do without him? I kept this information to myself.

Weeks passed and my father was still at the house. The thought of him leaving was stressful. I got high every day with Cameron. I stopped going to class and just started hanging out. The thought of my father leaving us put my stomach in knots. I smoked weed daily to ease the stress.

Things were getting back to normal. My father was home every day. My mother got back to her normal self; it was business as usual for everyone else except me. I couldn't get past the fear of my father leaving. I continued to smoke. I had missed so much class, I was way behind; I wasn't sure if I was going to be able to catch up. Shannon was my best friend and I hadn't shared with her what I was going though.

Months passed and my father was still home. I started to feel better. I would eventually have to tell my mother that I might not pass the tenth grade.

The weed stopped me from stressing, but it slowed me down and I wasn't getting anything done. One day, I was lying in my bed and I heard this voice talking to me. The voice told me to pull myself together and stop getting high. A week passed and I just didn't have the desire to get high anymore.

I was out from under the dark cloud that I was living under.

I started going back to class and I asked my teachers for make-up work. My mother was smiling again. My sisters were still annoying and my brothers were on my nerves. Our household was back in order and it felt good.

I had done a good job of catching up on all my missing assignments. Cameron and I remained friends; we just didn't get high together anymore. We were very attracted to each other, but I no longer got high. I knew if that one common denominator wasn't there, the relationship wouldn't work.

⇒ ⇒ ⇒

Life was good. I was still in contact with Bryce. He was coming home for Easter break. I couldn't wait to see him. Things had changed so much since he left. I would be turning sixteen in a couple of months.

My father worked hard during the week, but he always enjoyed a good cocktail on the weekend. It was Saturday and we were preparing for a family barbeque. It would be good to see my aunts, uncles, and cousins.

It was early in the day and I was in the kitchen helping my mother prepare the food. My father had started drinking already so he was a little tipsy. He was in a very good mood. He had Al Green playing as loud as it could go. My sisters were dancing around and my brothers were cleaning up the backyard before the company arrived.

The phone rang, and I stopped what I was doing to answer it.

"Hello."

"Hello Stormi. How are you doing? I'm still waiting for you to come and visit. I don't live too far from you. I think it's time for you to meet your little brother."

My heart started to beat fast, but I kept calm. I walked on the other side of the wall with the phone. I recognized the voice. It was that crazy bitch Babette. I was not going to let her upset my mother's day. I listened to what she had to say and I let her think I couldn't wait to meet my little brother.

I asked her for her address and the dumb bitch gave it to me. *Did she really think I wanted to have something to do with her?* I told her that I would come by and visit in a couple of days.

My father was dancing around in the kitchen with my mother; they were having a good time. My mother asked me who was on the phone.

"It was Shannon, Mom. She wanted to know what time we were getting started."

I hated to lie to my mother, but I was not going to let this backyard bitch destroy my family's day. *What was my father thinking when he stepped outside of his marriage?* Now this crazy woman is claiming she had his baby. Surely he couldn't be that stupid.

They call me Stormi.

Chapter Seventeen

All was quiet on the home front. There was no sign of Babette. I had her address so I planned to pay her a visit soon. My mind was on Bryce. He was on his way home. He would be arriving at three o'clock, and it was already two. He would phone me when he made it to the house, and I would be on my way to see him.

We had so much to talk about; it had been almost two years. The time went by fast and he kept his promise. We remained friends. I could always call him if I needed advice. I couldn't wait to see him. I had been dreaming about this moment. I didn't think he would have a problem with the jewel box this time, as my age was no longer a factor. I would be sixteen when he came home for summer break. I hadn't had sex with anyone. After that fiasco with Jermaine, I hadn't dated anyone. Well, I guess you can say I dated my hand—the one good thing James taught me to do was masturbate. I could always give myself a good nut! I'm ready to make love to Bryce; I was counting the minutes of his arrival. He was going to be a jewel box-kissing brother. I was getting wet just thinking about it.

The phone rang.

"Hello."

"I'm home!"

"I'm on my way!"

I made it to Bryce's house. I was excited, as I ran to his door.

"Bryce, let me in."

Bryce opened the door and I jumped in his arms. I gave him the wettest tongue kiss one could imagine.

"Wow, Stormi that was some kind of kiss. Girl, you're getting better."

"Baby, I missed you so much. I'm so glad you're home. I have been dreaming about this moment ever since you told me you were coming home."

I pushed Bryce on the couch and got on top of him, before I could get my clothes off, the door opened.

"Bryce, your aunt wants to know what you want to eat."

"Okay, hold up Stormi, I want you to meet someone,"

I turned to see a tall, beautiful brown skinned chick with a red dot in the middle of her forehead, she had long silky black hair past her shoulders, and she looked like an Indian.

"Stormi, I want you to meet Aasha."

"Hello, Aasha."

"Stormi, we finally get to meet. Bryce talks about you all the time."

"Really, well, he has never mentioned you."

"Oh that's okay; he would have eventually gotten around to it."

What is going on and who is this bitch? I was feeling irritated, but I tried to remain civil.

"Stormi will you be dining with us?"

"No, Aasha, I won't be dining with you all. I just stopped by to welcome Bryce home."

"Okay hopefully, before we return to school we can all go to dinner."

"That sounds like a plan Aasha. Well, Bryce it was good seeing you, welcome home. I will talk to you later."

"Okay Stormi I will give you a call."

I got in the car and left. I was so confused. *If I didn't know any better, I would think Bryce and Aasha were a couple.* My feelings were hurt, not because he might have a girlfriend, but because he didn't think enough of me to tell me.

Stormi 2: Don't start tripping; it is what it is. He is not your man and he doesn't owe you any explanations. Pull your shit together and move forward; we still have to deal with Babette, don't give that bitch a pass.

I decided to go over to Shannon's house. Things were different now that she had a baby. She couldn't go out like she used too, but she seemed okay with it. I often wondered if King knew that the baby was his. I saw him occasionally walking down the street. He still ain't shit. Shannon never mentions his name, but there would come a time when she would have to tell her daughter who her father was.

I knocked on the door. Shannon opened the door with her daughter Joy propped on her hip.

Joy was a beautiful baby girl with hazel eyes and blonde hair. She looked nothing like Shannon or King. No one in Shannon's family had colored eyes and King didn't have colored eyes either. He was just ugly. *I guess you never know what you might get when you mix pretty and ugly together. Thank God, Joy didn't look like King.*

"Hey Shannon, what are you up to?"

"Girl nothing, just sitting around playing with Joy. Let's go to my room; we can listen to music and talk."

"Okay."

"Stormi where have you been?"

"I went to see Bryce."

"Oh, is that the older guy you told me about?"

"Yes that's him. I go to his house; I was so excited to see him. I was kissing all over him and in walks this Indian-looking chick. She introduces herself to me. Her name is Aasha. She had the nerve to ask me if I would be dining with them. She attends the same school Bryce does."

"Did Bryce ever mention her?"

"No, he didn't, but Aasha told me he had told her all about me. I find it strange that Bryce never mentioned her and even stranger that he didn't tell me he was bringing a guest from school to stay at his house."

"Well Stormi, he really doesn't owe you an explanation. He's not your guy."

"I know he's not my guy, but we have been friends for a long time and we tell each other everything. I think he should have mentioned her."

"Stormi you sound jealous."

"I am jealous. I know I don't have any reason to be, but to be honest I thought he would be spending his time with me. I feel hurt, but I will never let him know."

"I'm sorry you are upset. Just look at the bright side."

"There is no bright side, Shannon. I'm done with everybody. I need to get me a job and try to make me some money. I would like to have my own car by the time I turn sixteen."

"Where do you plan on working?"

"I'm going to put an application in at McDonald's. I hear they are hiring."

"That sounds like a good idea. Working will keep your mind occupied and you won't have time to think about Bryce. I wish I could work, but taking care of a baby is a full-time job, but I can't complain; she is a good baby. I have to take her for a checkup on Friday. The appointment is after school. Since you're her godmother, would you like to go with us?"

"That sounds like a plan. How are we getting there?"

"My mother is going to let me borrow the car so we don't have to ride the bus."

"Okay."

With all that had happened with Bryce, the week had gone by quickly, it was already Friday. I was looking forward to going to my goddaughter's doctor's appointment. Shannon and I met up after school and we ran home to get Joy.

We entered Shannon's house and her mother was sitting on the couch with Joy. She had a wet towel on Joy's head.

"Mom what's wrong with Joy?"

"Shannon, I'm not sure. She has been hot all day. I gave her baby aspirin, but it doesn't appear to be working.

I was waiting for you to get out of school so we can take her to the hospital."

"She already has a doctor's appointment, let's go."

Shannon wrapped Joy in a blanket. Her mother got the car keys, and we headed to the doctor's office. Joy looked very pale and she was extremely hot. We got to the doctor's office and they saw her right away. Shannon's mother and I sat in the waiting room. Shannon came out to tell us what was going on.

"They drew blood; we are waiting on the test results. Joy is resting. I am going back in. I just wanted to let you all know what's going on."

I said a little prayer for my goddaughter; I knew that she would be okay. "Father God, please put your arms around precious little Joy. I pray that you heal her body. I thank you in advance for your blessings."

A couple of hours had gone by and we were still waiting. Shannon ran into the waiting room to let us know that the doctor was having Joy transported to the hospital. Her blood test came back and she needed a blood transfusion.

What was happening? She was just fine the other day. She

was playing and smiling and now she had to be transported to the hospital. This was crazy!

The ambulance arrived and the Shannon left with Joy. Mrs. Roberts and I followed the ambulance to the hospital.

We were sitting in the hospital waiting room, waiting for Shannon to give us an update. In walked Mr. Roberts, he sat next to Mrs. Roberts. Shannon entered the waiting room with tears streaming down her face. Her mother jumped up to see what was wrong.

Shannon told us that they tested her blood and that she was not a match for Joy. She needed another donor, preferably the father. Joy had a rare inherited blood disorder that causes her bone marrow to stop making enough new blood cells for her body to work normally.

My eyes grew big. Shannon had never divulged to anyone who the father was. Shannon pulled me to the side and told me to go and find King and tell him he needed to come to the hospital.

"Are you sure, Shannon?"

"Yes I'm sure. I'm not going to let my baby die, because I don't want people to know who her father is. Get on the phone and call James; he will know how to find King."

Shannon went back to the nursery to be with Joy. She never said a word to her parents. Mr. and Mrs. Roberts confronted me. Mrs. Roberts grabbed my arm.

"Stormi who is Joy's father?"

"King is Joy's father, Mrs. Roberts."

Mrs. Roberts fell back into her seat. Mr. Roberts took me to the nurse's station to use the phone.

"Stormi, do what you have to do to find him. Does he even know about Joy?"

"No, Mr. Roberts, he doesn't, so it's going to take some convincing to get him here."

"If you have a problem getting him here, you let me know and I will send some friends of mine to pick him up and they won't be nice about it. You tell that motherfucka to get here and save my grandbaby!"

The first person I called was Reese. I knew she would know how to find King.

"Hello Reese, this is Stormi."

"Who?"

"I don't have time for your dumb shit, I need you to find King and have him come to Dominquez Valley Hospital."

"For what! Why are you calling me?"

"I'm calling you because I don't have a number on him and I know you know how to reach him. Shannon's baby Joy is in the hospital and she needs a blood transfusion; she is extremely ill."

"What does that have to do with King?"

"Reese you know he's the father."

"Oh my God, I didn't know that. I thought she got pregnant when she went to Arkansas."

"No, she left pregnant."

"Okay, Stormi this is serious. I will try to locate King, but I don't think he will come."

"Why not?"

"That would be admitting that he had sex with a minor."

"Well when you talk to him; you tell him he better come or Shannon's father is going to have his crazy friends pick him up and they will hurt him."

"I will do my best. I will bring him myself."

"Okay thanks."

Hours passed, and Shannon entered the waiting room, she wanted to know if I had found King. I explained to her that Reese was looking for him and she would bring him to the hospital when she found him. Shannon paced the floor. Her mom and dad were trying to talk to her about King. Shannon wouldn't give them any information. She told her parents that he was the father and that was all they needed to know.

Shannon went back to be with Joy. I sat with my head in my hand. I was trying to make sense of what was going on. I felt a tap on my shoulder. It was Reese, and King was standing right next to her. Shannon's father grabbed King by the throat and damn near choked him to death. James ran in and pulled Mr. Roberts off of King. King was on the floor gasping for air. Mrs. Roberts jumped up and took King to the back to have his blood tested.

Reese took a seat and James had the nerve to try to hold a conversation with me.

"How are you doing, Stormi?"

"I'm good James."

"This is some crazy shit; Shannon's baby is too pretty

to be King's baby. We all thought she got pregnant when she went to Arkansas. King can't believe it's his; I had to make him come."

"Well, thanks for making him come. It's his baby. Shannon was pregnant when she left going to Arkansas. Did you forget King raped her?"

"Stormi, King didn't rape her. Stop spreading that lie. She was a willing participant.

"Fuck you, James!"

King came back to the waiting room and sat down next to James. James asked him what happened.

"I have to wait an hour and they will let me know if I'm a match."

"What do you mean 'if you're a match'? Why wouldn't you be a match?"

"Stormi, I don't think Shannon's baby is mine. She looks nothing like me."

"Whatever King, Shannon was a virgin when you raped her."

"I didn't rape her, Stormi. Close your mouth; you will get me hurt. Her father is just waiting to bust my head."

"Someone should bust your head."

The doctor entered the waiting room, but Shannon wasn't with him. Everyone stood to hear what he had to say.

"I'm looking for King McCoy."

"I'm King McCoy."

"Unfortunately, your blood was not a match for baby Joy. We appreciate you wanting to be a donor, but I thought I explained to Shannon that we needed the father not a friend."

"Are you saying that I'm not the father, Doctor?"

"No, Mr. McCoy, you're not Joy's father."

They call me Stormi.

Chapter Eighteen

King was not Joy's father.

King, Reese, and James started walking out of the hospital. King looked back at me with a smirk on his face. I gave him the middle finger. I hated that rat bastard!

Shannon's mother pulled me to the side to talk to me.

"Stormi, I want you to tell me what's going on. When Shannon found out she was pregnant she told me she wasn't sure who the father was. I didn't ask any questions. Joy gets sick and King shows up to give blood. Now we find out King is not the father. What is going on?"

"Mrs. Roberts, I am just as confused as you are. You're going to have to talk to Shannon about this."

Stormi 2: It appears your friend has some explaining to do. If King is not the father then who is? Your so-called best friend made a fool out of you. You had her back and she was lying to you. Trust no bitch! So how did Joy get here? It must have been by Immaculate Conception.

Mrs. Roberts sat down to talk with her husband. I needed to find out what was going on so I went to the nursery to talk to Shannon. I walked into the nursery and Shannon was holding Joy, rocking her in the rocking chair. Shannon looked at me and whispered, "Give me a minute." I stood in the hallway, waiting for her to come out.

Shannon walked out of the nursery with tears rolling down her face.

"I already know Stormi. I have no idea what's going on. King was the only man I had sex with and I swear on my daughter, that's the truth. The doctor ran the test twice. They are one hundred percent sure King's not the father."

"Shannon, Joy has a father. Maybe you blocked him out of your memory."

"Stormi, the only other guy I was seeing was Tony and we never had sex!"

"You had sex with someone, because you have a baby; I think you have blocked it from your memory. Maybe you need to see a therapist and they can help you recall. What will happen if they can't find a donor?"

"If they don't find a donor for my baby, she will die."

"Well, let's find out who the father is."

"And how are we going to do that?"

"We are going to sit down and go over every inch of your life during the time you and King had sex."

"Stormi, before today you would always refer to King as the person that raped me. Now he's the guy I had sex with. I have no reason to lie to you; don't stop trusting me now. You are my best friend. If I knew what happened I would tell you."

"I'm sorry Shannon, the story is just so unbelievable I really don't know what to believe, but I'm going to trust you and we will work through this together."

Shannon's mom walked into the nursery. She wanted to sit with Joy. While she sat with Joy, Shannon and I went to the cafeteria to get something to eat and create a time-line for Shannon. We had to try to jog her memory.

Shannon and I sat down at the table to make sense of what was going on.

"Shannon, how many people have you been intimate with, not including King?"

"Stormi, before King violated me I was involved with Tony, but we never had sex. We messed around, but we never went all the way."

"What does "messed around" consist of?"

"He never penetrated me."

"Okay, well what did you guys do?"

"We did a lot of grinding and rubbing and finger bang-ing, but he never put it in, but he did nut on me."

"Did you have your panties on or off?"

"My panties were off."

"We might have to consider Tony as Joy's father."

"There's no way he could be the father. We never went all the way."

"Shannon, I believe that you may need to contact him. It won't hurt to try."

"Yeah and tell him what? I think you may be my baby's father, even though we didn't have sex! He's going to think I'm crazy."

"He can think what he wants, but for Joy's sake we have to try. It's the only thing that makes sense.

Mrs. Roberts came to the cafeteria to get Shannon. The doctor needed to speak with her in regards to Joy's treatment. Shannon returned to the nursery and I was left to sit with her mother.

"Stormi, you have to tell me what's going on. I can't help Shannon if you all don't tell me what's happening. Shannon never told me she knew who the father was and based on what has happened today, she actually doesn't know who Joy's father is. Joy gets sick and King shows up here to be tested and then come to find out he's not the father. What the hell is going on?"

"Mrs. Roberts, you have to ask Shannon what's going on. It's not my place to tell Shannon's business."

In walked my mother. She talked to Mrs. Roberts and then she told me it was time for me to go home. I knew we were going to have a long talk on the way home. This was the second incident with Shannon—first she tried to commit suicide, and now the person she thought was her baby's father isn't. I was back in the same situation as before. Should I tell my mother what was going on or not.

I guess the old saying, *what you do in the dark will eventually come to the light,* was true. No matter how hard we tried to avoid telling what happened with King, the truth was still going to be revealed, and to add to the drama Shannon didn't know who Joy's father was. It could be Tony, the person she never had sex with. I was so confused. I couldn't wait to get home and go to bed.

I went to the nursery to let Shannon know that I had to go.

"Shannon, my mother is here to pick me up, but I will be back in the morning. Is there anything that you need?"

"Yes Stormi, I need you to get Tony to come to the hospital to get tested."

"Shannon, I think this is a conversation that you need to have with him. I don't think I'm the person to convince him that he may be Joy's father."

Shannon got very upset and started to cry. "I don't know what I'm going to do if we don't find a donor for

Joy. I know there's no other person that could be her dad; I just have to make him understand."

"Maybe you should get some professional advice. Let's ask a doctor if it's possible for you to have gotten pregnant without penetration. If the doctor says it's medically possible this will convince him to come and be tested. I hate to leave you, but my mother wants me to come home. I promise I will be back in the morning."

I left the hospital so worried that Joy might not make it through the night. I felt like it was all a dream. Why was this happening to Shannon? One day she was playing and singing to her daughter and the next day her daughter was lying in the hospital fighting for her life.

Stormi 1: Pick up your Bible and pray. Prayer changes things. Read Psalms 56:3-4 "When I am afraid, I will trust in you. In God, whose Word I praise, in God I trust; I will not be afraid."

I made it home; it had been an extremely long and stressful day. All I wanted to do was take a hot bath and go to sleep. I lie in my bed thinking about Joy. I got up and got my Bible and I searched for something to read that would make me feel better. In walked my mother.

"Do you need anything, Stormi?"

"Yes Mom, I need you to pray with me. I'm so worried about Joy. I can't sleep."

"Okay Stormi, we are going to pray. Father God, I come before your throne asking for forgiveness of any sins we have committed knowing and not knowing. We stand in the gap for baby Joy. You said in your word Matthew 18:19: *That if two of you shall agree on earth as touching anything that they shall ask, it shall be done for them of my Father, which is in heaven.* We are asking for a donor for baby Joy and a full recovery, in the name of Jesus we pray, Amen."

I felt so much better after the prayer. I just knew that God was going to make away for Joy. I was not going to worry, as I knew God heard our prayers.

It was early Saturday morning and I was up and ready to go back to the hospital to visit Joy. I had a good night's sleep and I felt great. I could give Shannon a break. I woke up my mother and I asked her to drop me off at the hospital.

I got to the hospital and Shannon was feeding Joy.

"Good morning, how is she feeling today?"

"She's doing much better today, but she still needs a donor. I did talk to a doctor about my situation, and he told me that there's a very good chance that I got pregnant without penetration. The only way I will know is if Tony comes and gets tested."

"Well I can stay with Joy and you can go home and take a bath and try and reach Tony."

"That sounds like a plan. My mother is on her way back. I will have her take me home. Thanks for being such a good friend, Stormi."

"Shannon you're my best friend. We ride or die together. I will see you when you get back."

Shannon left the hospital. I sat in the rocking chair, holding Joy. She was hooked up to an IV and a monitor. As I rocked her, I looked at her face. She looked like an angel. Joy was one of the most beautiful babies I had ever seen; she really did have an angelic face. She had the most amazing eyes and sandy brown hair, but it looked blonde sometimes. I rocked Joy for about an hour. The nurse came in to take Joy for more tests, letting me know she would be back in the nursery in about an hour. I went to the cafeteria to stretch my legs and get something to drink.

Thirty minutes had passed before I headed back to the nursery. When I got off the elevator, Shannon and her mom were standing at the nurse's station.

"What's going on? You have only been gone an hour."

"I spoke with Tony and he came back to the hospital with me. He's at the lab being tested."

"That's great. I'm so happy for you. He didn't put up a fight?"

"There was some resistance, but I showed him a picture of Joy and his mother pulled a picture out of Tony when he was a baby and she looks just like him — blonde hair and all — and to top it off, Joy has colored eyes like his mom. We just need the blood test to finalize everything."

"Shannon, did they bring Joy back from testing yet?"

"No the nurse said she should be back in about an hour; that's just enough time to get Tony's results."

While waiting for Tony's test results, I said a little prayer and thanked God for blessing baby Joy with life. I knew deep down in my heart that Tony was the father.

The elevator door opened and Tony was standing there with this big crazy grin on his face. Shannon ran over to him.

"What did they say, Tony?"

"I am Joy's father. Now let me meet my daughter."

Everyone was jumping up and down, screaming with excitement of the good news. Shannon was on her knees praying and thanking God for the blessing, as tears of joy ran down her face. Tony helped her up and they went to the nursery to wait for Joy to return. This was one of the happiest days of my life. I know without a doubt that I will always pray. God is a good God!

Several hours had passed and Joy was still not back. Shannon went to the nurse's station to see what was going on. The charge nurse told Shannon she would be in to talk to her. They were changing shifts and she had to get updates on all patients.

Code blue! Code blue! Dr. Mitchell, please report to Pediatrics ICU. Code Blue!

"Shannon is Dr. Mitchell Joy's Doctor?"

"Yes."

They call me Stormi.

Chapter Nineteen

This was such a sad day.

We were having Joy's service at her gravesite. Shannon refused to have her service at the Chapel. I had been with Shannon every day since Joy passed away. She had not shed one tear. I knew that she was in shock, she had been running full speed ahead. She planned the service all by herself. She didn't want help from anyone. I knew eventually the reality of Joy's death was going to hit her, and I wanted to be there for her to help her through this hard time. Shannon's parents hired an attorney to sue the hospital for wrongful death. The nurse that took Joy down for more testing took the wrong chart with her, and

Joy was given a CAT scan. She was allergic to the Iodine and she went into cardiac arrest.

"The Lord giveth and the Lord taketh. Bless it be the name of the Lord. We are gathered here today to say farewell to our little angel, Joy. She was with us for a short time. It's never easy to bury a young child, but I want you to know that God is a God of restoration. He will mend your hearts and turn your sorrows into brand new tomorrows." The pastor finished his sermon and Shannon was preparing to read a letter she wrote to Joy.

My darling baby girl,

I knew when we first met that you would be my world. Your birth was effortless — no pains no strains — you came through my birth canal with ease. I knew then that life with you would be very sweet. You were so beautiful. I couldn't imagine that I had given you life. I knew you were a blessing from God because He told me so. I knew that you were my angel sent from above; I had already planned our life together when you were taken from me. I miss you so much, I can't sleep and I can't eat, the pain at times just seems unbearable. I can't image life without you. I had so much I wanted to teach you. You just started walking and you called me mama. I don't know if I can bear life without you. I guess God had a plan for our life. I remember going to the abortion clinic to get rid of you and they tried three times, but I woke up every time. On the third try, God spoke and told me to allow you to live. I never thought that you would leave me so soon, but I still thank God for allowing me to meet you and to be your mother for a short period of time. Until we meet again, just know that I love you with all my heart and we will see each other soon.

Love, Mom.

Shannon walked over and kissed the casket. She laid a yellow rose on it. She hugged and kissed her mother. She hugged her father, and she thanked everyone for coming. She walked over to me and hugged me tight.

"Stormi, you are my best friend and I love you. We have been together through thick and thin and I appreciate you. If Joy would have lived, I know you would have been the best godmother. My life will never be the same without Joy. She was my heart and soul and without her, I'm dead!"

I reached out to hug Shannon, but there was a different look in her eyes. I could see that she was no longer mentally here. Shannon took a revolver out of her purse and held it to her a head.

I pleaded with her to give me the gun.

"Shannon, you have so much to live for; please don't do this!"

Shannon's mother and father begged her to put the gun down. People start running to their cars, they were afraid that she might start randomly shooting.

The pastor held up the Bible. "Satan, I plead the blood of Jesus against you!"

Bang!

One shot to the head and Shannon was dead.

They Call Me Stormi.

Chapter Twenty

S tormi, you have been here for twelve months and you still tell the story as if it were yesterday. You ask me every day to sign your release papers. I need to know, with no uncertainty, that you are ready to go back out into the world and live your life."

"You still think I'm crazy, doctor. I have good sense. There is nothing wrong with me. I'm not a danger to myself. I know this shit didn't happen yesterday, I'm fully aware that my best friend took her life twelve months ago. She blew her goddamn brains out... But I'm locked up because I'm supposed to be crazy. This is some backwards shit.

"You motherfucka's lock me up because I wouldn't let them clean her blood off of me. Yeah, I wore her brains in my hair for two weeks. I let her blood dry on my face. I wore the same clothes for two weeks and my panties begged me to take them off. The pastors always say there is life in the blood. I was covered with so much of her blood; I wanted to see if she was going to come back to life.

"You keep me locked up because you don't think I'm stable. *Fuck you.* I'm more stable than you will ever be. *I'm the motherfuckin Storm, haven't you heard!* It's time for you to release me; there is no more blood on my face. I'm not crazy; I'm fully aware of what's going on. I'm not suicidal. You keep me locked up to get my parents money. If you don't release me soon I'm going to release havoc on your funny looking ass."

"Nurse please administer 2cc's of Ativan; the patient is becoming agitated."

Stormi 2: The doctor is not going to release you if you keep acting crazy. It's time to get out of here. Play nice on his next visit, participate in-group, and let's walk out of here, we got things to do.

⤜ ⤜ ⤜

"Welcome home Stormi."

"Hello Asia, did you miss me."

"Yes, I missed you, but people were saying that you went crazy. Did you go crazy?"

"Do I look crazy to you?"

"No."

"Don't worry about what people say, as long as you know the truth, fuck what they talkin' about."

"Hi, Stormi."

"Hey, Valencia, I sure did miss you always trying to take care of me. What you been up to?"

"Nothing Stormi, I've just been waiting for you to come home. I prayed for you every night."

"You don't have to pray for me. I'm good! I don't need prayers. I can handle my own shit."

Stormi 2: Calm down, you're getting to aggressive. They will lock yo' ass back up. Stay cool.

Everyone was tiptoeing around me as if I were going to break. I wished they would just treat me normal. I guess it was going to take a minute before they were comfortable with me being home. The one thing I missed while I was away was a Zorba's hamburger. I called Joyce to see if she wanted to go get a burger.

"Hello, may I speak to Joyce?"

"Who's calling?"

"It's Stormi."

"Hey, Stormi, it's Jackie. They let you out the crazy house?"

"Yeah bitch, they did, and guess what? I'm still crazy. You dumbass backyard bitch, I don't know who let you off your leash, but if I were you, I would get back into my doghouse. Be careful what you say to crazy people, you never know what they might do. Now let me speak to Joyce."

"Hi, Stormi."

"Hey, Joyce, you want to walk to Zorba's with me I want a hamburger?"

"Sure, I will be waiting outside for you."

"I walked down the street and Joyce was waiting for me.

"Hey, girl, what did you say to my sister? She's acting all scared of you. She told me to be careful; she said you're crazy as hell. I just start laughing."

"Fuck yo' sister!"

We make it to Zorba's and I see Trent.

"Trent how's it going?"

"It's going good. Your name is Stormi, right?"

"Yep that would be me."

"I heard you took a little trip."

"I sure did, but I'm back."

"So how you doing?"

"I'm good, I'm glad I ran into you, I need to make some money."

"Well, I'm the man you want to see. What you talking about doing?"

"I'm going back to school tomorrow and I want to start selling whatever you got."

"Well, I have black mollies and weed, which one do you want?"

"I want both."

"You think you can sell both?"

"Yeah, I can sell whatever. I need to have my own money. I don't want to depend on my parents anymore. I can sell the uppers to the jocks and the weed to the other fools. Just tell me how it works."

"Well I will start you out with 60/40. I will keep forty percent of what you make and you keep sixty percent. When you get good at it, I will do 80/20 and when you want your own product, you make one hundred percent."

"That sounds like a plan."

"Okay Stormi, I will meet you outside the gate at your school in the morning to give you a book bag. Everything you need will be in the bag."

They call me Stormi.

Chapter Twenty-One

I spent my entire eleventh grade in the crazy house, but I came out with a 4.0 GPA.

I had been back in school for six months and I was making more money than some grown folks were. Trent had taught me the tricks of the trade, and I was preparing to put my own crew together. Money made the world go-round; whatever you needed, if you had the money you could make it happen. Three of my teachers were on my payroll and I had two students taking care of my other classes. I could do the work but sometimes the medication that the doctors put me on made me move slow.

I decided to smoke weed. I felt better when I smoked weed. My nights were short. I still woke up to Shannon blowing out her brains with me standing there soaked in her blood. The weed allowed me to make it through the night.

Stormi 1: What an awesome God we serve. He is a way maker and a mind regulator, give it to Him and watch Him turn your gray days to brighter days. God loves us. He just wants us to have faith and He will do the rest.

I had to pay Trent a visit; it was time for me to have my own product. I needed to be in business for myself; no need to share my profits. I wanted to expand my location. I was going to let my brother Derrick start selling for me and my cousin Brittany. I needed to get my product at Trent's price.

Stormi 2: Yes, let's make this money; it's time for you to be on Trent's level. He likes you; use that to your advantage to get what you want. You know how this works. The jewel box is your way maker, you don't have to give him the box just give him a small piece of jewelry he will be satisfied with that.

It was time for me to settle with Trent. He picked me up after school.

"Baby girl, how you doing today?"

"I'm good; my money is good, your money is good, so that means we good! But we do need to talk. I need to be at that one hundred percent mark and I need it at your price."

"Damn baby, I'm not going to make any money if I don't step on the price just a little."

"Trent I've been hustling for you for six months. You have tripled in sales. I have teachers on payroll. When I leave school, I will graduate with a 4.0 and I will be able to buy whatever I want. I have money set aside so that I can take care of my sisters and brothers. I'm seventeen and by the time I'm eighteen I will be able to get my own place. I need yo' price."

"What are you willing to give me if I do that for you?"

"What do you want?"

"Girl, you know what I want."

"Check this out, I don't play games. My jewel box is full of expensive treasures; you need the key to look, and the only way you will look is if I'm getting the product for free. Until then you get to smell and taste only!"

"I can deal with that!"

Stormi 2: This is going to be like taking candy from a baby. If you give this fool some two-day-old panties to smell and a taste test, you will have him where you want him in no time.

Business was booming. I had my cousin Brittany and my little brother Derrick on the money train.

I finally got Trent to give me his price. All I had to do was give him a taste of my jewel box. I actually didn't mind; Trent was a fine brother!

They only person that had ever laid any pole was James and he was not in the picture anymore. I just might consider letting Trent get a ring or two out of my jewel box! I liked the way Trent operated, but I didn't think it was wise to mix business and pleasure. I was going to take my time and see how things worked out.

☙ ☙ ☙

The money train was on the move. Brittany was doing a very good job selling at Worthington High. I was waiting at the park for her to get out of school. As I sat waiting on Brittany, I calculated what I had in my stash. I should be able to get my car by graduation.

Brittany walked up and she had some guy with her.

"Hey Stormi how you doing?"

"I'm doing good. How you doing, Brit?"

"Things are good; this is my friend Justin."

Justin was a fine brown-skinned brother with curly hair. He was about six-foot-two, slim, and muscles in all the right places. He had a wonderful smile with beautiful white teeth. This dude was almost pretty! I couldn't take my eyes off him. *Shit!*

"Hello Justin, my name is Stormi."

Justin nodded.

Brittany and I took a walk and she left Justin sitting on a bench.

"Brittany, what's the money lookin' like?"

"Girl, we did very well. I sold out. I'm on my way to the mall when I leave here to go shopping."

"Don't overdo it with the shopping. Be very careful how you spend money, people are always watching you. Don't want to make it obvious that your finances have changed. Your mother buys you all that high priced shit anyway, so just be careful. So what's up with Justin, is that your new boyfriend?"

"Girl no, Justin and I have been friends for a long time. His parents moved to Louisiana a couple of years ago and now they are back. I haven't seen him in a couple of years. He's like my brother."

"I'm happy about that because his ass is fine!"

"Stormi, I thought the only thing that moved you is your money!"

"Well, that is true, but Justin would be a good distraction. Does he know what kind of business you're in?"

"No."

"Keep it that way."

Brittany and Justin were leaving, and he nodded his goodbye.

It had been a long day. I was at Trent's house to get more products.

"Stormi, baby, have a seat. I will be with you in a minute. I have some new product for you; I want you to tell me what you think."

"What is it, Trent?"

"My supplier turned me on to hash; it's real nice. You stay high longer so you don't have to smoke as much. Let's try it together."

"It's just weed, right?"

"Yes, it's just weed. I wouldn't give you anything else."

"Let's do it."

Trent and I sat on the couch and fired up the hash. It was a smooth smoke. Five minutes later, I felt like I was floating on a cloud. We listened to the smooth groove of The Isley Brothers. *Make me say it again girl, make me say it again girl. You're all I need, oh yes you are.*

Trent set the mood and I moved right with him. He kissed me from the top of my head to the soles of my feet, taking his time as he took my body to a new level of ecstasy. I was in trouble! We were eye to eye. Trent had beautiful brown eyes with an Asian look to them. His chocolate smooth skin was flawless and he had a shadow for a mustache. He took the melted wax from a candle and poured it on me. What the....

This was a new experience; my mind was floating in the air. Was it the hash or was I really feeling this dude? Damn, here comes the massage; this dude was rubbing me down. He had my jewel box dripping, and everything was in slow motion, but still no entrance to the jewel box.

He had me wanting him badly. He kissed my jewel box tenderly and got up.

"Was I just mind fucked?"

"What was that Trent? You're not going to finish?"

"Baby girl, I want you so bad, but I just have to take my time with you. Stormi I have feelings for you. I'm not going to misuse you. I want to give you every inch of me. You're so precious. Your beauty and intelligence intrigue me. I want to be yours. I think we will make a helluva team. You and I together; there are no limits."

Wow, did this dude get smooth on me. I couldn't believe this; I wanted to fuck and he was mind fucking me. This was the second time I had encountered an older dude and he left my jewel box dripping like a leaky faucet. What the hell! *Somebody fuck me please!*

They call me Stormi.

Chapter Twenty-Two

I had my mind on my money. My money team was doing their thang. My little brother Derrick was a hustler. We were definitely cut from the same cloth. By the time I leave Corona High, I would have set the pace for him. I would be moving on to bigger and better thangs.

Trent was a good dude. We had been spending a lot of time together. He had been covering everything for me—my entire product was free! I was not sure if this was a wise decision. I knew that nothing in this life was free. Everything had a price, and I knew that one day he was going to want to cash in. Just the other day he told me, he loved me. What the hell! How could he love me? After all this time, he still hadn't put his pole nowhere near me.

He would kiss my jewel box all day long, but he refused to lay that pole of life. Whatever, I was going to ride this money train until the caboose fell off. "I got my mind on my money."

I had been hanging out with Brittany and Justin; I liked that dude. He was book smart, almost a nerd type. He had his life all planned out, all he talked about was going to college. That's where we differed. I never considered going to college. School ain't my thang. I wondered if he knew I liked him. I gave him hints all the time, but he never seemed to get them.

Brittany and I were going to his track meet today. I was tired of just being his friend. I wanted more from him and Trent wanted more from me. My obvious choice should have been Trent. We had a good working relationship and I was sure he could make my jewel box sang! However, there was something about Justin that gave me butterflies in my stomach. He was a chance at a safe life. He represented peace and calmness. I had no one to talk to. Hell, I spent the majority of my time with Trent. I wasn't even hanging out with Joyce anymore. We saw each other from time to time but she was not someone I would tell my secrets. I had no one to laugh with, and no one to cry with.

I borrowed my mother's car to take a trip to the cemetery to visit Shannon. I needed to talk to her. I had a strange feeling that someone had been following me. It just might have been my imagination. That fuckin' medication was bullshit, sometimes it made me have crazy thoughts, but then again I thought it might have been my girl Shannon trying to communicate with me. I find Shannon's grave site and I sit and talk to her.

"Shannon, I wish you were here. I miss you! Why did you leave me? My life has never been the same. When you killed yourself, you killed me too. Why would you blow your fuckin' head off in front of me? Did you even consider what type of impact that was going to have on me? I was the one that found King raping you. I was the one that found you when you hung yourself. I was the one that sat at the abortion clinic with you. I was the one that stayed by your side when they said King was not the father. I spent a year in the crazy house wondering if there was something that I could have done that would have changed this outcome. I know you wanted me to kill myself too, so we can be together in Heaven. You bitch! I know there has to be a method to your madness. Your plan almost worked. I considered taking my life many times, but something kept me from doing it. Every time I thought about taking my life, the strangest thing would happen. I would feel a cold wind blow across my body, now mind you, I would be indoors. This has happened to me before; I would cry out, 'God, Is that you?' I never got an answer, but the feeling of taking my life disappeared.

"Suicide is a major sin. We learned that early in Sunday school. I don't know if you made it to Heaven, I hope you did, but I can't leave this earth until God says so. We will forever be best friends and your death and Joy's death won't be in vain. I promise you that. There will be *No Mercy!* for those who have harmed you! So stop following me around. I feel your spirit hovering over me."

Stormi 1: You have to trust God; he is forever present with you! He is concerned with your wellbeing, Psalm 34:4 I sought the Lord, and he heard me and delivered me from all my fears.

Psalm 34:7 The angel of the Lord encamps all around those who fear him and delivers them.

Stormi 2: Did you take your meds? Smoke a joint, you are head tripping. Get it together and go to the track meet. You need something to get your mind right!

I fired up a joint!

"Here's to you Shannon. I can only stay thirty more minutes. I have to go to a track meet. Oh yeah, I forgot to tell you. I met a new guy; his name is Justin. He's so smart and all he talks about is going to college. Did I mention that he is fine! I think you would like him. He is different from the other guys I have been with. I'm sure you would approve."

It was time for me to go to the track meet. As I got up to walk to the car, it felt like someone was following me, but I didn't see anyone. I got into the car and as I got ready to start the car, I noticed a red lily on the windshield.

The track meet was great. Justin came in first in the 100-yard dash and his relay team came in first. We were celebrating at the pizza parlor. Brittany and I reserved a room for Justin and his friends but Justin didn't know I paid for everything. Everyone was having a good time. The music was playing and people were everywhere. Brittany and I were sitting in a booth watching the festivities. Justin slid into the booth, and sat next to me.

"Thanks for coming to my track meet, Stormi."

"You're welcome, I had a good time. You're really fast."

"Yes, I have been competing for a long time. I was hoping to get a track and field scholarship to go to college."

"You're really serious about going to college, huh?"

"Yes I am. You're not going to college?"

"Well, I haven't really thought about it. I thought it was too late to apply; we only have six months left in school."

"You can still apply. If you want, I will help you."

"Okay. That would be great."

"I will come by your house next week and we will get started."

Why didn't I just tell him, I didn't want to go to college? I will just go through the motions with him. This way, I will get to spend time with him. We sat for a couple of hours just laughing and having a good time. I hadn't had fun like that in a long time. I sat back and watched my peers; everyone was so carefree. It appeared that they didn't have a worry in the world. All I could think about was how to make the next dollar.

⇒ ⇒ ⇒

I lay in my bed thinking about what a great time I had hanging out. I hadn't had a social life since I had been home. It's all about making money. I really liked Justin; he made me feel alive. I couldn't stop thinking about him. I needed to get my mind back on my money. Ooh, but that Justin sure made me smile.

Stormi 2: It's nice to dream, but Justin is not your speed. Call Trent and see what he's up too. School will be out soon and he will be on his way to college. It makes no sense for you to get your hopes up high. He won't be around for long.

I got up to get a glass of water. As I reached the kitchen the phone rang.

"Hello,"

"Tell yo' daddy I'm not finished with him."

"What did you say, bitch I will—"

Before I could get another word out of my mouth, I was listening to the dial tone. What was going on now? I had been gone a year. I know Babette was not still fuckin' with my family. Asia would have told me if she was. *Could this have been someone new?*

⸙ ⸙ ⸙

Justin was a man of his word. He came over and we filled out applications for several colleges. We spent hours going over what the different colleges had to offer. Justin really had me believing I could go to college. After we finished, Justin ate dinner with my family. It was a good day!

Justin was ready to leave and I walked him to the door.

"Stormi, I really enjoyed your family. I had a good time."

"Thanks Justin, I appreciate you helping me with my applications."

"No problem. With your grades, I'm sure you will get offers from more than one school. Stormi, I wanted to ask you about prom. I don't have a date for prom and I was wondering if you would be my date."

"Really?"

"Yes, I have wanted to ask you for some time now, but I thought you had a boyfriend."

"No, I don't have a boyfriend. Of course, I will go with you."

"Okay, that's good. I have to go. I will call you tomorrow."

Justin kissed me goodbye. My heart was beating so fast. I couldn't wait for tomorrow.

Stormi 2: Stop with the bullshit, you are not going to college. Stop wasting Justin's time. We have plans already and they don't include your new little boyfriend. You're getting off track!

❧ ❧ ❧

The phone rang at 7:00 am.

"Hello."

"Where have you been?"

"What do you mean?"

"Stormi, I haven't seen you in a couple of days. What's going on?"

"Trent, I can't spend every waking moment at your house. I do have a life!"

"Will I see you today?"

"No! I have shit to do. I don't need any product; I'm good for now."

"I need to see you today!"

"For what?" I was now irritated.

"Because I miss you!"

"Trent, I will see you later. Why are you acting as if we are together?"

"Stormi, we are together. I'm the one that gives you your product free. I'm the one that rubs you down when you need me to. I'm the one that makes sure no one on the streets mess with you. Little girl, do you think you would make the money you make if I didn't allow it? I do all of this because I care about you. Now all of a sudden you don't have time for me. What's going on?"

"Nothing is going on. I don't see you for a couple of days and you act as if the world is ending. This is the thing. I have been thinking about my life. I'm not sure I want to always hustle. I'm thinking about going to college."

"Stormi, you don't have to hustle. I make enough money for the both of us."

"Trent, it's not about the both of us. We are in business together. We don't have any commitments. We have fun together. That's all. We are friends with benefits. I think I need a change and I believe going away to school will give me a new start."

"Stormi, you can go away to school. I will go with you. Whatever you want to do, I will support it. I just want to be with you. Don't you know that I love you?"

"Trent you just don't get it. I don't want to be tied down. I'm too young. I need to figure out who I am. I'm not ready for a commitment."

Click! He hung up.

Months had passed and my life had changed dramatically. Justin had been a great influence on my life. We are officially a couple. God is good! I was back in church, I was accepted to Florida State University, and Justin will be attending as well. I couldn't believe how God had blessed me. I was so angry when Shannon died; I had vowed never to go to church again. I was now on the right track. I stopped selling drugs.

I tried to make things right with Trent, but he wouldn't have anything to do with me. He would pass down my street from time to time and I had seen him lurking around at Justin's track meets. When I tried to approach him, he would leave. Someone phoned the house every day and hung up, and I still had a strange feeling of being followed. Just last week there was a different flower left on the front steps of my house for five days straight.

The first flower was an orchid, the second flower was an orange blossom, the third flower was a primrose, and the fourth flower was a flower they call sweet pea and last but not least, a red spider lily. It was all so confusing until Justin did some research on the flowers.

The orchids meant love. The orange blossoms meant eternal love. The primrose meant "I can't live without you" and the sweet pea meant goodbye and the red spider lily meant death.

My parents were sure Babette sent the flowers. They went to the police station to file a restraining order against her, again. I knew in my gut that Trent was behind this. My biggest regret was getting my little brother Derrick involved. When I decided to stop dealing with Trent, I sat down with Derrick to let him know we were no longer in business. He refused to stop selling; he said the money was too good. There was no way I could guarantee Derricks safety if I was not involved with Trent.

I went to visit Trent early Saturday morning. I had to convince him to forgive me and to watch my brother's back.

When I arrived at Trent's house, it took him a very long time to answer the door. I knew he was standing on the other side of the door, watching me out of the peephole. I could hear him breathing hard. After a ten-minute stand-off, Trent opened the door and walked away. I followed him to his bedroom. I begged for his forgiveness. I tried to explain to him that I wanted to live a different life, one of peace and calmness. I told him college was going to give me the new start I needed. For once in my life, I needed my life to reflect my actual age. I no longer wanted to live the life of an adult. I wanted to take my time and grow up. I begged him to take care of Derrick. I told him that I was my brother's keeper and I came to guarantee his safety in the streets.

Trent walked up to me and started removing my clothes. I stood in the middle of the floor naked. He walked over to his stereo system, and put on an album by the O'Jays "She Use to Be My Girl" started playing.

Trent went to his kitchen and returned with a bottle of honey. He took the honey and dripped it all over my body. I stood in the middle of the floor covered in honey!

Trent removed his clothes and stood in front of me like a chocolate Adonis. I watched his pole of life stretch out towards me. I could see his heart beating out of his chest. I didn't know if this was a sign of passion or anger, as he moved towards my body, breathing heavily. I began to shake uncontrollably. Trent sucked my nipples until they stood at attention. He grabbed me by my hair and threw me on the bed.

He kissed my body all over, paying special attention to the inner parts of my thighs. He lay on top of me to make entrance into my jewel box. "Ooh wee" his pole of life stroked my jewel box with so much intensity. "Yes" I shouted, as I reached an orgasmic climax that left my body weak. I almost told him I loved him, but I knew it was just the sex making me feel that way, so I didn't say a word.

I got dressed to leave. Before I could get out the door, Trent took me by the hand and whispered in my ear. "I'm your brother's keeper."

I smiled and walked away.

They call me Stormi.

Chapter Twenty-Three

The prom was two weeks away. I was excited; my mother had my dress made. Justin was coming over to make sure his tuxedo matched my dress. The doorbell rang, its was Justin.

I opened the door and Justin walked in the house. He had the biggest smile on his face.

"Why are you smiling so hard?"

"No reason, I was just thinking time is winding up and we will be graduating next month."

"I know I can't wait."

"By the way Stormi as I was getting out my car there was a lady standing in front of your house. I asked her if she needed some help and she said no. I asked her who was she looking for and she said, "I'm just standing here admiring my house. My son's father lives here and I will be moving in soon." I told her, "I think you have the wrong house." She looked at me with a smirk on her face and walked away. Before I could ring the doorbell, some dude in a '64 Chevy Impala stopped in front of your house, he called me by my name. "What's up Justin?" he said. I asked him "Do I know you?" He told me to tell you that Derrick inherited your debt and then he drove off."

"What!"

"That's what he said."

"Where is Derrick? Has anyone seen Derrick?"

"He was walking up the street when I was getting out of my car. He should be in front of the house by now."

"Oh, okay."

"What's wrong? What debt do you have? And who was that lady?"

"It's nothing; don't worry about it. I just need to talk to Derrick."

While I was talking to Justin, I heard a loud sound.

Bang! Bang! Bang!

I turned to Justin and asked, "Did you hear gunshots?"

"I sure did."

I ran toward the front door with Justin running behind me. My heart was racing so fast. I felt like my heart was going to jump out of my chest. When I got outside, my worst nightmare was staring me in the face. I did not want to believe what my eyes were seeing. Derrick was lying face down in front of the house. He had been shot. My body was paralyzed; I couldn't move. There was blood everywhere. Asia ran outside to help Derrick. She turned him on his back to see if he was breathing.

Derrick screamed, "Stormi, it was…"

Asia laid her body on top of him to keep him warm. Asia cried out to God to save him. When I finally came around, I ran to help Asia with Derrick; she was performing CPR on him.

"Breathe, Derrick!" I shouted.

"Stormi, get out of my way. I got this! You're slowing me down!" Asia shouted.

As Justin helped me to my feet, I noticed a red spider lily soaked in Derrick's blood.

Stormi 1: God is your peace! **In the Midst of the Storm.** *His peace surpasses all understanding.*

They call me Stormi.

Chapter Twenty-Four

❧

"S tormi, it's time for group session," my psych thera-pist said.

"I will be there when I get there." I answered in a hostile tone.

"Stormi, the doctor is not going to tolerate you not attending group therapy."

"Bitch, this not my first rodeo, I will come when I get good and damn ready. Stop fucking with me."

I was angry. I wanted to do something bad to somebody, anybody, and everybody. I was in no mood to sit in a group session. I needed to express what I was feeling, but I did not want to express my feelings in words. In fact, I could not express what I was feeling in words. I felt like if these motherfuckin' people knew what I was thinking;

they would have my ass strapped down immediately. I was expressing my thoughts by writing on the mirror. I was thinking about all the people that had fucked with me. I wrote the words, "NO **MERCY**" in large red letters.

My therapist asked, "What have you written on the mirror?"

I snapped at her saying, "Bitch! What does it look like?"

"Stormi, you are defacing hospital property. You need to erase that right now." She tried to use her psychotherapy bullshit on me by saying, "Okay, let's look at what made you choose the words "NO **MERCY**" And what's going on in your mind as you write? As you know, writing can be therapeutic."

Stormi 2: Stop fuckin with these people, you know the routine. It's time to get out of here. Play nice, and go to the group session, and tell the doctor what he wants to hear. I have been workin' on this hit list since you were thirteen. Revenge is going to be a motherfucka!

They call me Stormi!

≈ ≈ ≈

"Now I lay me down to sleep, I pray the Lord my soul to keep."

The storm is quiet, but just for a sea-
son. The storm will return!

Coming soon, the sequel,

NO MERCY!